ÂF421571

KEN SANCHEZ

No Matter What

Copyright © 2023 by Ken Sanchez

All rights reserved. No part of this publication may be reproduced, stored or transmitted in any form or by any means, electronic, mechanical, photocopying, recording, scanning, or otherwise without written permission from the publisher. It is illegal to copy this book, post it to a website, or distribute it by any other means without permission.

This novel is entirely a work of fiction. The names, characters and incidents portrayed in it are the work of the author's imagination. Any resemblance to actual persons, living or dead, events or localities is entirely coincidental.

First edition

This book was professionally typeset on Reedsy.
Find out more at reedsy.com

Contents

Acknowledgement

To those who believed in me, thank you. Also, gay rights!

Trigger Warnings

This book contains references to hate crimes and violence.

1

David

"ARE YOU SURE YOU WANT TO DO THIS?" David's best friend and the current person he can't have because he's straight, Ryan Evans, chimed in as they waited for their coffee in a local Starbucks in London.

Ryan had become a stubborn fixture in David Miller's life, a relentless headache that just wouldn't quit. Then again, he was also the secret crush David had been nursing since their teenage days. That was a whole fifteen years ago, and now they were approaching the grand age of thirty.

David really should have moved on from his crush on Ryan ages ago, but somehow the man just kept getting better with age. Ryan had turned into a towering six-foot-five hunk of a bodybuilder, and on top of it all, he was a ginger. Red-haired men were David's personal kryptonite, if he were being all poetic about it.

Meanwhile, David's own transformation was a little less dramatic compared to Ryan's. He was now a positively towering five-foot-eleven, boasting some truly average blue eyes and a body that could be classified as "okay." Ryan had been attempting to drag him to the gym where he worked, but David couldn't envision himself getting all sweaty and worked up there. He figured he was doing decently in the body department, thank you very much.

But today, oh today, David was on a mission to finally pull himself together and take a swing at that never-ending crush on Ryan. He'd even gone as far as setting up a date with a guy who went by the name "BodybuilderBarbie" on Grindr. They'd been chatting for a couple of days, and they'd finally managed to find a slot in their schedules to meet up. It had been a hot minute since David had dated, probably because his last relationship had ended in a spectacular disaster. That, of course, was why Ryan was being overly protective.

Why can't I have you instead, David mused in the secret corners of his mind.

"Yes, I am sure. I think it is time, Ry," David affirmed, though there was a hint of uncertainty in his voice.

"I won't be able to stop you, will I?" Ryan sighed in reply.

"Nope," David said, letting that 'p' really pop.

"Oh, come on, at least take me along," Ryan playfully pleaded.

David wasn't exactly sure what game Ryan was playing, but it was definitely cute. It had also somehow managed to cross over into the territory of borderline annoying. He kind of wished Ryan's concern came from a different place rather than just pure, plain worry.

Exhaling another sigh, David gave in, "Ryan, it's a date. Just two people enjoying each other's company. If you tag along, it's going to be more of a threesome situation, and you know how I feel about those."

"Fine, just promise to call me when you're done, okay?" Ryan relented.

"I promise. Pinky swear?" David said, his voice dripping with playfulness despite their adult status.

"Two orders of Pumpkin Spice Lattes for David!" the barista called, and David collected their drinks, handing one over to Ryan.

"Why do you even like this stuff?" Ryan said, sipping from the cup despite his grumbling.

The hypocrite, David thought with a grin.

"Complain all you want, but deep down, I know you secretly love it more than I do," David replied, raising an eyebrow.

Ryan muttered something under his breath, but David was too busy pretending to be a basic latte-sipping cliché to catch it.

"Sorry, what was that?" David asked, a mischievous glint in his eye.

"Nothing, I said where to next?" Ryan deflected with a smirk.

David shrugged, deciding to let the previous banter slide for now.

"We're going shopping, and you're going to be my fashion consultant for this date," David announced with an authoritative tone.

"D, you know I couldn't care less about clothes," Ryan sighed dramatically. Only Ryan could get away with using a nickname like that and making it sound like pure, unadulterated seduction.

Stop it, he's straight.

Sure, David knew that fact well, but who said he couldn't have a little fun?

"Your job is simple, just nod and say yes to the dress. Got it?" David instructed with a grin.

"Yeah, yeah," Ryan agreed with a mock groan, the playful smile lingering.

David affectionately ruffled Ryan's hair. "Good boy, now let's roll."

Their destination was the Westfield in Shepherd's Bush. It was David's holy grail of shopping centres, offering everything he could ever dream of.

Their first conquest was Ted Baker. David's status as a stylist for A-list celebrities meant he could be a little generous with his clothing budget.

David eyed a stylish button-up that would perfectly complement his chest. True, David wasn't the epitome of traditional masculinity, but Ryan had often teased that he could easily pass for straight.

Fuck that! David scoffed inwardly.

Speaking of Ryan, the man sat there looking like a sulky cloud as he sipped his latte. And then it hit David—an idea so brilliant that a mental lightbulb practically lit up above his head. It wasn't often that lightbulb got turned on, but when it did, interesting things were bound to happen.

David pulled a handful of clothes from the racks, the ones he thought would make Ryan look irresistible, and deposited them into a basket. Once satisfied, he sauntered over to Ryan, all mischief and charm, and hauled him to the fitting room.

"David! What in the world are you up to?" Ryan exclaimed, his surprise genuine.

"Don't question it, just try these on," David said with an air of mystery, pushing the basket into Ryan's hands.

"But I can't afford any of this!" Ryan protested.

"Who said you're paying? And why are you so riled up?" David teased, enjoying Ryan's flustered state. "Just try them on, alright? I'll be out here, waiting to witness the magic," David said with a wink, leaving Ryan to his fate.

Returning to browsing clothes for himself, David was snapped out of his thoughts when Ryan finally emerged from the fitting room.

David's jaw promptly hit the floor, and he was pretty sure he could hear a symphony of gasps from the other patrons.

"So, how's it looking?" Ryan asked, rubbing the back of his neck sheepishly.

Ryan looked beyond incredible. If David were a woman, he would have dropped to one knee and asked for Ryan's hand in marriage right then and there. Dressed in a snug coat over an unbuttoned shirt, showing off his chiseled chest, and those pants... well, they left absolutely nothing to the imagination.

"Like sex on legs," David managed to utter after a moment of stunned silence. "Good lord, I amaze even myself. Now, come on, give the rest of those clothes a spin so we can work out the bill."

Ryan, blushing like a schoolboy caught stealing cookies, obliged and treated everyone present to an impromptu Ryan Fashion Show. Spectators chimed in with their opinions, and while Ryan was clearly embarrassed, he was definitely lapping up the attention.

After Ryan had transformed back into his original attire and handed over the chosen items, they made their way to the checkout counter. David thoroughly enjoyed playing the role of the generous friend, something that wasn't always feasible while they were growing up.

Exiting the store, David suggested, "We've got a bit of time to kill. How about a quick visit to my parents' house?"

"Absolutely, your parents are a hoot," Ryan agreed.

David's parents were a fantastic pair. He had come out to them when he was fifteen, and his Dad's response had been to hand him a condom with a stern warning not to impregnate anyone. His Mum had been equally entertaining, advising him to wait until he was eighteen before getting busy with men. David loved them dearly.

Their home was tucked away in a quiet corner of Ealing, West London. While it might have been perpetually damp, it exuded a peaceful serenity that made up for any gloominess.

Taking the central line of the tube, David and Ryan embarked on their journey to Ealing. It was the final stop on that particular route, and it was pretty much impossible to miss. Despite the occasional chaos that could ensue on the London Underground, both David and Ryan had a soft spot for it, valuing its efficiency and quirkiness.

In order to get to his parents' house, they still had to walk for a couple more kilometers, and they didn't mind it one bit. They loved to walk and just talk about random nonsense.

They passed the Broadway, and Ryan practically had to drag David away from buying bubble tea. David definitely had an addiction to those drinks, so Ryan was right to haul him away. If it got any worse, he would have to join BubbleTea-Anonymous, which David thought wasn't a real thing.

Or is it? Maybe he should research, he thought.

They were walking through Walpole Park when Ryan spoke up again. The park was beautiful in a peaceful sort of way. Stepping inside felt like going through a movie scene. It was currently summer in London, so there were some people around who were half-naked. David didn't mind it as he honestly encouraged it. A little bit of eye candy can't hurt.

"So, what is this guy like?" Ryan asked as they walked in the cacophony of trees.

"Why are you so invested in my love life all of a sudden? Don't tell me you're jealous?" David teased.

"Look, I just want you safe, okay?" Ryan said seriously.

David stopped teasing and answered his best friend honestly. "He's nice. Handsome. Has blonde hair and grey eyes."

"That's it?" Ryan said perplexed.

"Did I mention that he was hot?" David asked.

"Are you going on a date or a one-night stand?" Ryan raised an eyebrow at him.

David thought that he didn't deserve to be shamed for his dating habits.

"Ryan! Are you shaming me?" David clutched his imaginary pearls.

"Fine, do whatever you want. It's not like I can stop you anyway," Ryan said as he started walking faster.

David caught up to him and turned him around. "Where did this come from? Are you okay? You don't normally act like this."

"Nothing, I am sorry, okay? I don't know why I snapped at you like that. Just stressed, is all," Ryan replied.

David wasn't buying it but decided to let it go.

"Hey, you know I am here if you need me, alright? You don't have to suffer on your own anymore," David said softly.

"Okay," Ryan said, and he hugged David.

Ryan's parents passed away when he was a kid. He grew up with his grandparents who never really paid any attention to him. Ryan was the introvert who always preferred to suffer alone than to voice out what was troubling him. David saw this immediately and managed to get Ryan out of his shell. David didn't know why his friend was going back to that shell at this moment.

"Come on, Mum told me she baked us cookies," David said when they broke apart.

"White chocolate chip?" Ryan asked like he was a little kid again.

"Yes, they love you more than me sometimes anyway," David said, and they carried on walking.

They finally arrived at David's parents' house. It was a two-story house in the middle of Ealing. Like any houses in the UK, it was made out of brick and lacked air conditioning. They really needed it, especially during the scorching summer times. Right now, David was already sweating, but when he turned, Ryan seemed to not be sweating.

David's Mum came running and gave them all hugs. He needed to visit them more. After getting a job and growing up, he was able to get a place in Knightsbridge, close to Harrods. Ryan had been at him to visit his parents more, but his job took priority these days.

"Hey Mum, where's Dad?" David said as they finally broke the hug.

"Hey son, Ryan. Come on in. Your Dad is in the kitchen finishing up," David's Mum, Irene, said.

His parents owned a bakery in town that was a hit with the locals. David's Dad, Lucas, was the baker of the two and David absolutely loved it when he baked for them. His Mum, on the other hand, was the better cook. It was late in their life that they realized they wanted to open up a business, so David took it upon himself to help them do it. It was nothing compared to what he put them through growing up.

Upon entering the kitchen, David could immediately smell the cookies that his Dad was baking. David saw him checking on the oven.

"Hey Dad! Are the cookies ready?" David was giddy.

His Dad stood up and gave them both a toothy grin. "David! Ryan!" Lucas hugged them both like his Mum did. "The cookies will be done shortly. Why don't you two help and set up the table?"

They both nodded eagerly and helped out before sitting down.

"So what brings you two here today?" His Mum asked.

"David is going on a date tonight with a complete stranger," Ryan said, and David stared daggers at him for ratting him out.

"Is this true, David?" His Dad said, sporting a concerned frown on his face.

David sighed. "Yes, I just thought it is time for me to get out there."

His parents knew about his crush on Ryan, so it was normal for them to be concerned when someone mentioned that he was dating again.

"Where is this man taking you?" His Mum chimed in.

David looked at Ryan for a second, then to his parents. "He's taking me to Heaven, Mum."

"What?" Ryan was shocked.

"Why are you mad? It is where gay people go to have fun and sometimes date."

"You couldn't have told me this beforehand?" Ryan was mad.

"Relax, I'll be back before you know it, okay?" David placated Ryan.

"Who's going to take care of Tyson?" Ryan asked.

Tyson was David's cat. David took him from a rescue centre and fell in love with him ever since Tyson licked his face.

"About that, can you look after him for me? Pretty please," David pleaded.

David saw his parents looking at them with a look that he couldn't decipher.

"Fine. That way I can still clean up your mess," Ryan grumbled.

David hugged him. "Thank you!"

His parents laughed at their banter, making them pull away from each other.

"Alright, you two, enough of that," his Dad said as he took the cookies out of the oven and placed them on the table. "Now eat. You have a big day today."

The cookies ran out after five minutes.

<h1 style="text-align:center">2</h1>

David

"TYSON, WHAT DO YOU THINK?" David asked his cat. "Do I look hot enough to eat?"

"Meow," Tyson said.

"Good boy." David crouched down to pet his cat on the head. His cat wasn't wrong though, he looked great. *Narcissist much?* he thought, but who was he kidding. You can't live life without a bit of it.

David was wearing a beautiful suit that he had bought earlier with Ryan, and he had a deep v-neck shirt underneath, along with muscle-tight trousers that made his ass pop.

His house in Knightsbridge was not that big considering the prices here were astronomical. He was able to snag the one he was in because he had hooked up with one of the realtors.

Yes, he was a bit of a slut back in the day, but a man had to live.

David heard his doorbell ring and immediately stopped admiring himself.

David sighed. "Come, Ty. Uncle Ryan is here." He crouched down and gently picked up Tyson.

David headed to the door and opened it to see Ryan looking absolutely delicious in a tank top, jacket, and a pair of joggers.

Damn, can this man not be hot, please?

"Ry, come on in. You got here a little early," David said after a moment of being stunned, shocked, and possibly hard.

"You look… great," Ryan said as he walked inside.

"You think so?" David was surprised. Ryan rarely gave him compliments. The moon was probably blue outside.

"Yeah. You know that already, so there's nothing new there," Ryan said.

"Well, thank you. Come on, have a seat. I made some tea," David said.

Ryan followed him to the kitchen where David was brewing some tea. It might not be bubble tea, which he liked so much, but his tea was the next best thing. Oolong infused with honey, delicious.

He poured a cup for Ryan and handed it to him. Ryan generally loved his tea even though he kept telling David that he was a coffee person.

"You and your fancy tea," Ryan chuckled, and David poured himself some as well.

"You drink it anyway," David quipped, earning another chuckle from Ryan.

"Are you nervous?" Ryan asked.

"A little. You know how I get before meeting someone," David said.

Before his last relationship, David had been an unstoppable dating machine. Anxiety be damned. He managed his work and dating life consecutively. But the asshole had given him a lot of trauma and never really paid for it. His confidence had taken a deep dive into the Bermuda Triangle.

"Look, for what it's worth, if I were into guys, I'd be dating you instead," Ryan said.

"Well, you still could. I mean, who's stopping you?" David knew the reason why, but he wasn't going there.

"You know, Elle would come up here and tear your shit up," Ryan said.

Of course, the girlfriend. Elle "The Devil" Rion was the annoying woman Ryan was stuck on. David didn't know why he was still with her, but being the friend that he was, he let it happen.

"Why are you still with that woman?" David blurted out suddenly and froze.

Ryan raised his brow at him. "I'm sorry? Weren't you the one who introduced us?"

"Yes! But I didn't think you would actually like her! I didn't even know her that well when I introduced you two," David replied.

David had met Elle at a party once and she pestered him to bring her to another party where he had already invited Ryan. He was regretting it now.

"She's not that bad, but I get it. She can be too much at times," Ryan sighed.

"I'm sorry, I didn't mean to say that out loud," David said after a while. He really was sorry about it. He didn't mean to put his friend down.

"It's alright, mate. I appreciate the honesty." Ryan put his empty mug down and proceeded to hug David.

Ryan smelled good. David could just bask in his scent like a wolf on heat, but he had to stop it before his trousers got even tighter.

David pulled back and took both their empty mugs to the sink.

"Alright, I have to go. Are you going to be okay?" David asked.

Ryan picked up Tyson, who was purring under him. "Yeah, me and this little guy will have some fun tonight."

"Be good, you two." David chuckled and headed to the door.

As soon as he got out of the door, David immediately texted Mr.BodyBuilderBarbie to check if they were still on for their date. He got a reply a minute later, with his date only saying the word "Yes." Sometimes David felt like talking to a brick was better.

He took the tube since he didn't own a car. Owning a car in London was useless. The traffic was so bad that a forty-minute journey could turn into a five-hour drive. David didn't have the time for that, and besides, it was just another expense that he couldn't afford.

He got out of Embankment station just an hour before their meet-up. He texted his date again and waited for a response.

Most people in London, especially in the gay community, knew about the place called "Stairway to Heaven." It was a place that anyone could go to before entering the club.

David decided to do just that. Couldn't hurt to get some drunken courage before his date got there.

The bar was currently packed with patrons, and considering he came to this bar pretty often on a Friday night, he knew most of them. After getting past all of the nosy people, he was finally able to get to the bar. He smiled as soon as he saw who the bartender was. It was his good friend Layla, who was a badass lesbian. He came to the bar often enough that they were able to create a good friendship.

"Hey, sugarplum," Layla said. "You're here early today. What can I get you?"

"I have a date tonight and you know me, the usual, please," David replied as he watched Layla make his drink.

"A date, huh? Does Ryan know about this date?" Layla asked as she put his beer in front of him.

Ryan and Layla had gotten acquainted when David brought him to the bar. Ryan loved it, and Layla and he had become instant friends. David was glad that he had been able to share a part of himself with Ryan.

"Yeah, he does. He's currently cat-sitting Tyson at the moment. He loves that cat more than he loves me," David said. Layla went back to serving customers, but he knew that she could multitask and was listening to his loud mouth.

"You know he loves you more than your cat. You're just being your dramatic self again," Layla said when she came back and took the money for his beer. He tapped his watch to the card machine and paid for it.

Man, technology is amazing!

David sighed. "I know. I just wish that he was gay."

"You never know, people can surprise you," Layla winked at him as the bar started getting busy.

He looked at his phone to see if the guy had responded, but he never did.

He had been at the bar for at least two hours, and he was just now realizing that he had been stood up.

Not going to lie, he was a little drunk. He was on his sixth beer, and he would have gone for another one if Layla hadn't stopped him.

He called her over as he was about to leave. "Layla, I'm going," David said. He slurred his words, so he probably said something gibberish.

"Do you want me to call you a cab?" Layla offered, which was incredibly nice of her.

David waved her off. "No, no, it's fine. Don't bother."

Layla looked skeptical, but she nodded at him before he waved goodbye.

He got outside and felt the fresh summer air go through him. It wasn't pleasant, but it would do.

He began walking back to the station before he realized that it was already close to midnight.

Fuck.

David walked around to get to the road but before he could get there, he was grabbed from behind. His heart was beating fast as he didn't know who grabbed him.

"Stay still, or I will knife your guts out." David froze and stopped fighting. "Boys, we got another one those queers in here." He heard the man say.

"Don't hurt me, please. I was just heading home." David pleaded but that didn't seem to work.

The group of men laughed and one of them David saw had a face tattoo that resembled a cross. "You think you're getting out of here you disgusting queer." The man spat at his face and punched his stomach.

David fumbled and his vision began to get blurry.

The man took a portion of his hair and pulled his face up. "This will put you in your place!"

He took another hit to the back. David tried to get away but someone struck his legs with a bat and he tried to scream.

The man who was holding him shut him up with his hand. "Shut up! Go ahead and end it boys."

I am sorry, Ryan. I love you. No matter what.

That was the last thing he thought of before getting hit in the head with a baseball bat.

3

Ryan

"WHERE IS HE?" Ryan asked himself.

He tried calling David's phone for the umpteenth time, but he wasn't answering. This wasn't like David, as he normally answers Ryan's calls.

He tried again, but it just went to voicemail.

Tyson was in his lap, purring loudly when he received a call an hour later. He answered it without knowing who it was.

"David?" Ryan said.

"Ryan? It's me, Irene," David's Mum said. Ryan could hear her crying, as well as Lucas sobbing in the background.

"What's going on? Why are you crying?" Anxiety was getting to him at this point.

"It's David… He… He was…" Irene tried to say, but he heard Lucas take the phone from her.

"Ryan, listen to me. You need to get to St. Thomas' Hospital now," Lucas said, and he ended the call.

He didn't waste any time and took an Uber to the hospital.

Please, David. Please be okay.

Ryan sat in the back of the Uber, his heart racing in his chest. Worry consumed him with each passing moment. The streets of London rushed past, a blur of lights and traffic.

The phone call played over and over in his mind. Lucas and Irene's voices had been urgent, and fear had twisted Ryan's stomach

When the Uber arrived at St. Thomas' Hospital, Ryan quickly paid the driver and practically jumped out of the car. He hurried through the entrance, his heart now pounding even faster. The hospital's sterile scent engulfed him as he followed the signs to the reception desk, desperate for any information about David's condition.

His mind was a whirlwind of worry, a mix of fear and hope. All he yearned for was to see David, to hold him close, and to find out that he was okay.

"Hi, I am here for David Miller. His Dad, Lucas Miller, told me to come here," he said urgently.

The nurse looked at him sadly, but Ryan didn't know what that meant, and he didn't have time to think about it. All he wanted to think about was David.

"Alright, he's still currently in surgery, so you can head into surgery room three, and you'll find them there," the nurse said softly.

Ryan felt a sinking sensation in his chest upon learning that David was in surgery. Fear consumed him as he hurried toward the surgery ward, each step feeling as though he were moving through dense fog.

Upon reaching the surgery ward, he noticed David's parents and Layla, their faces etched with worry. It was heart-wrenching to see the people he cared about most gathered there for David. Ryan knew he had to be strong for them, especially for David himself.

He attempted to hide his own anxiety behind a reassuring smile, but the tight knot in his stomach refused to loosen. The waiting room seemed suffocating, filled with the collective unease of everyone present.

Ryan located an empty chair and sat down, his hands fidgeting nervously. His only wish was to be there for David when he emerged from surgery.

Finally gathering the courage, Ryan asked, "What's happening?"

David's parents were too upset to give a clear answer, their voices trembling with fear. Layla, however, stepped in to explain.

With a heavy sigh, Layla said, "David's date left him alone at the bar, and when he left, someone found him hurt and bloodied in an alley."

Ryan felt a surge of anger and worry, but he realized it wasn't the time for questions or blame. He held onto the hope that David would recover, and they could face whatever had happened together, just like they always had.

"Why is David in surgery?" Ryan asked.

Tears streamed down Layla's face as she struggled to find the words. After taking a shaky breath, she managed to say, "When the paramedics arrived, I saw that David's head was injured, and it was bad." Her voice broke as she wiped away her tears with trembling hands. "I'm so sorry, Ryan. I should have been there for him."

Ryan's world felt like it was falling apart as he absorbed Layla's words. He couldn't believe what had happened to David, his best friend, his confidant, the person he cared about most in the world. The image of David hurt and bleeding in an alleyway haunted his thoughts.

Despite feeling shocked and overwhelmed by fear, Ryan reached out and put a comforting hand on Layla's shoulder.

"Layla, it's not your fault. None of us could have seen this coming," Ryan said, his voice shaking with a mix of sadness and anger.

In that moment, the waiting room felt like it was closing in on them, with tension and uncertainty making it hard to breathe.

Layla mentioned, "The detective will arrive once they're done at the scene."

Ryan's mind was filled with questions, each one more pressing than the last. Layla's mention of the detective sharing their findings only increased his curiosity. What had they found at the place where they found David? Did they have any clues about who had hurt him? Ryan's heart was heavy with worry, and he yearned for answers that could ease his anxiety.

He couldn't stop replaying the events leading up to this moment. David's date leaving him alone, the mysterious circumstances that had left him injured and stranded in that alley.

It all felt like a nightmarish ordeal from which he desperately wanted to wake up from.

As the minutes dragged on, Ryan struggled to hide his anxiety, but the uncertainty was eating away at him. He knew that the Detective's findings would provide clarity, but the wait was unbearable. All he wanted was to see David awake and safe, to hold him close and reassure himself that he was alright.

Yet, all he could do for now was hope and wait.

"How long has David been in surgery?" Ryan inquired.

Layla checked her watch and then met Ryan's eyes. "It's been around two hours."

Two hours. The mere thought gnawed at Ryan's nerves. He understood surgeries were unpredictable, and the longer David stayed in there, the more concerned he grew. Every passing minute felt like an eternity, and he couldn't shake that overwhelming sense of helplessness.

Ryan teetered on the brink of emotional breakdown, but he knew he had to keep it together for David and everyone else in the room. Time continued to creep by, and the surgery room remained eerily quiet, leaving them all suspended in uncertainty.

Ryan's anxiety reached a fever pitch as a man in a suit approached. He assumed this must be the Detective they had been anxiously waiting for. Rising from his seat, Ryan introduced himself and the others, his voice trembling with a mixture of worry and anticipation.

"Are you here for David Miller?" the man inquired as he drew near.

"I'm Ryan. These are David's parents and Layla. We've been waiting for an update. Can you please tell us what happened to David?"

The man extended his hand in greeting. "I'm Detective Wayne. I wish we were meeting under different circumstances, but I'll share the information I have. David was brutally attacked. He was struck in the head and knees with a baseball bat. We found the weapon in a nearby park, discarded after the assault."

Ryan's heart sank, struggling to process the horrifying details.

"A baseball bat? Why would anyone do something like that to David?"

"I'm sorry to say this, but we suspect this was a hate crime," Detective Wayne explained grimly. "According to an eyewitness, David wasn't a random victim; he was deliberately targeted."

"A hate crime? But David... he's never harmed anyone. Why would someone target him like that?"

As Detective Wayne's words hung heavily in the air, they were left with a bone-chilling realization that David had fallen victim to something far more sinister than they could have ever imagined.

"What about the person who did this to him? Has the guy been caught?" Lucas asked, his eyes burning with rage.

Detective Wayne's expression turned darker as he delivered the disappointing news. "Unfortunately, the person responsible got away, at least for now. We're still waiting for the nearby places to check their security cameras."

Ryan's heart sank at those words, a flood of emotions surging through him. The idea of David's attacker escaping justice was almost unbearable. He clenched his fists, trying to keep his cool.

"So, they just walked away after what they did to David? This can't be real," Ryan said, his frustration evident in his voice.

The Detective nodded, offering a sympathetic look. "I understand how frustrating it is, Ryan. We're doing our best to find the person responsible, but it'll take some time."

Ryan's mind raced, a mix of anger, despair, and helplessness swirling within him. He couldn't grasp how someone could commit such a terrible act and get away with it.

"We can't just let them off the hook. David didn't deserve any of this," Ryan said, his voice heavy with frustration.

As the harsh reality of the situation sunk in, they all felt an urgent need to seek justice for David. They shared a determination to ensure the person responsible faced consequences.

Unable to contain himself any longer, Ryan ran. He couldn't believe this was happening to one of the most important people in his life. He sprinted as far away as he could and let out a scream, not caring if others thought he was crazy. David was in there, fighting for his life, and Ryan felt utterly helpless.

Ryan found himself near the Thames, feeling utterly exhausted and drained. But he knew David wouldn't want him to feel this way. David wouldn't allow it.

He sat down on a bench and stared up at the sky. If he were a religious person, he might have prayed for David's recovery, but he knew better.

"Rough night?" someone next to him said.

"You could say that," Ryan replied, turning to see an elderly man sitting beside him.

"What's troubling you, young man?" the old man asked.

Ryan let out a sigh. "My friend got brutally beaten up, and now he's in surgery fighting for his life."

"That's a tough situation. Want some advice from an old man?"

"Sure, why not."

"I know it's tough to see right now, but things will improve. Your friend will make it through. And I want you to remember that you're not alone. We're all here for you. No matter what happens, you have the strength to get through this."

Before Ryan could express his gratitude, his phone rang. When he looked up after the call, the old man had vanished. He shook it off and answered the phone.

"Ryan? Oh, thank goodness. You should come back here. The doctor wants all of us to be there," Layla's voice conveyed the urgency of the situation.

"Okay, I'll be right there," Ryan replied, his heart racing with a mix of fear and hope. He hurried off, heading straight for the hospital.

Arriving at the hospital in record time, Ryan found David's parents and Layla anxiously waiting in the surgery ward. Their worried expressions mirrored his own concerns.

The doctor, both a source of comfort and dread, began to share the news. "Are we all here?" Their collective nods were filled with anticipation. "Good. Mr. Miller is currently stable." A collective sigh of relief escaped them, though Ryan couldn't ignore the lingering uncertainty.

"It took us some time, but we managed to stabilize him. The knee injuries were relatively minor. However, the blow to his head was quite severe." Ryan's heart sank, his hope held on even tighter. "There was some blood clotting in his brain, which we've drained. We can't be certain about the impact on his memory, but we're hopeful for the best. Right now, all we can do is wait for him to wake up." The doctor continued.

"Can we see him?" Lucas' voice trembled with anxiety, mirroring the group's eagerness.

"Yes, he'll be in the ICU. But only one person can go in at a time," the doctor explained before leaving.

"Ryan, you should go first. We want to see him, but we don't want him to see us like this." Lucas said.

Ryan nodded, touched by their consideration, and hugged them tightly. "Thank you. I'll let you know how he's doing." Turning to

Layla, he asked, "What about you?"

Layla glanced at David's parents, who were deeply worried. "I'll go with the Millers. He needs you more right now. Do you need anything?"

Ryan shook his head, feeling grateful for his supportive friend. "No, thanks. I'll be okay. Take care of yourselves. I'll call when he wakes up."

With that, Layla joined David's parents, leaving Ryan alone with his thoughts and the impending visit to the ICU.

A nurse guided Ryan through the sterile corridors of the ICU, her footsteps echoing softly in the quiet environment. His heart raced, a mix of fear and anticipation building inside him.

Following the nurse's instructions, he put on a hospital gown and latex gloves, his hands trembling slightly. With each step closer to David's room, the air seemed to grow heavier with worry.

Upon entering David's room, the sight before him nearly shattered his resolve. Tubes connected various machines to David's still body, and swathes of white bandages hid the extent of his injuries. The dried, rusty stains on David's face were a painful reminder of the violence he had suffered.

With utmost care, Ryan sat down beside David, his eyes scanning every bandage and tube. It was as if he believed his sheer willpower could heal the wounds.

He reached out and took David's hand, being cautious not to disrupt any medical equipment.

Tears welled up in Ryan's eyes as he pressed his lips to David's bandaged hand. "Please be okay. I need you. We all need you."

Ryan's shoulders shook with silent sobs, and he didn't care about the time or the nurses moving around the room. His entire world had narrowed down to this small, sterile space and the man lying before him.

The compassionate nurses draped a warm blanket over his shoulders. Hours passed like this, the machines humming softly, and the nurses murmuring in the background. Exhaustion tugged at his senses, his eyes weighed down with unshed tears. Still, he refused to leave David's side, determined to be there when his friend woke.

As weariness finally overcame him, Ryan drifted off to sleep, still holding onto David's hand.

4

Ryan

A SOFT RUSTLING SOUND STIRRED Ryan from his slumber. He blinked, kind of confused, then realized it came from David's bed. That jolted him wide awake, heart pounding with a mix of hope and worry.

Without wasting time, Ryan hit the call button to get the nurses over to David pronto. They came in fast, their faces hidden behind masks.

Ryan stepped back, giving them room to do their thing. He stood there, holding his breath, as they tweaked the tubes, checked the monitors, and turned the room into a whirlwind of activity.

David's eyes stayed closed, his face all peaceful. But underneath, there were signs – a tiny shift of his head, a small twitch of his bandaged hands.

Ryan stayed glued to the spot, not taking his eyes off David's face. It was marked by what he'd been through, but it was still the face Ryan cared about.

Time dragged on, each second feeling like an eternity, until finally, David's eyes fluttered open. Ryan's breath hitched, and he held still like he was afraid to break the moment.

David's eyes, roamed around the room. Ryan's heart swelled as their eyes locked, even if David wasn't fully getting what was happening.

Ryan couldn't help the tears that welled up, and he gave David a gentle smile. "Hey, David, you're awake."

Time hung heavy as Ryan waited, heart pounding like a drum.

He wanted to hear David's voice, see that recognition in his eyes. Instead, there was just a blank look, like David was trying to figure out a tough puzzle.

He wanted to reach out, hold David's hand, and tell him everything was going to be okay. But the tubes and machines kept David tethered to that sterile hospital bed, leaving Ryan feeling utterly powerless.

Then, something shifted. Pain flashed across David's face, a wince that spoke of discomfort. Panic surged through Ryan as the medical team jumped into action, moving like a well-oiled machine. The room buzzed with urgency, and Ryan's heart raced as he watched them work to ease David's pain.

The nurses managed to give David the meds he needed to relieve the pain. Slowly, the lines of strain on his face softened, and his breathing became steadier.

As the drugs took effect, David's eyelids drooped, and his gaze, which had been locked onto Ryan's, grew distant. Ryan leaned in, his fingers gently brushing David's cheek. "Rest now, David," he whispered, choked up with emotion. "I'll be right here, waiting for you to wake up."

The room settled into a quiet stillness, only broken by the soft hum of machines. Ryan settled into a chair beside David's bed, his eyes never leaving his sleeping form.

The door to the sterile room creaked open, and Ryan turned to see the doctor walking in, bringing with him that faint antiseptic smell and a load of uncertainty.

"Hey, Ryan," the doctor greeted him with a warm but cautious smile as he approached David's bedside. Ryan nodded in response, his anxiety simmering just beneath the surface.

The doctor got to work, checking David's monitors, going through his chart, and then shifting his attention to Ryan. Their eyes met, and there was something in the doctor's look that gave Ryan a glimmer of hope.

"Doctor, how's he doing?" Ryan asked.

He couldn't tear his gaze away from David, lying there so still, tangled up in all those tubes and wires.

Dr. Christiansen took a deep breath, "Ryan, I get your concerns. David's situation is pretty complicated, and it's only natural to want some answers," he began, speaking carefully. "Like I mentioned earlier, the head injury David sustained can mess with his memory and thinking."

Ryan's heart sank at the reminder. The idea of David not recognizing him, of all their shared memories slipping away, was a heavy weight on his mind.

The doctor went on. "Right now, we're in the early stages of figuring out what's going on. What we're sure of is that David's brain took a serious hit. The exact impact on his cognitive functions can vary and we won't know more until we run some more tests."

Ryan nodded, taking it all in, even though he was filled with uncertainty. It was hard to shake that feeling of helplessness, of not being able to reach David through the fog that seemed to surround him.

"So, what's the plan?" Ryan asked, his voice a mix of desperation and resolve.

Dr. Christiansen gave a sympathetic smile. "Right now, Ryan, just be here for David. Your presence can provide comfort, even if he doesn't realize it now. We'll keep a close eye on his progress."

Ryan let out a slow breath. He wished he could do more, offer the same kind of security that David had always given him.

"Thanks, Doctor," Ryan said, filled with gratitude. "Please, do whatever you can to help him."

With a nod, Dr. Christiansen left the room, leaving Ryan alone with his thoughts and the rhythmic hum of the machines watching over David's every breath.

After a while, he noticed David's parents just outside the room, peering through the large window. Their presence showed the deep love and concern they had for their son, and Ryan felt a deep empathy for them.

Ryan stood up from the chair beside David's bed, his footsteps muted on the hospital floor.

Irene turned her tear-filled eyes toward him, her voice shaky with worry. "Ryan, how is he? What did the doctor say?"

Ryan gave a reassuring smile. "The doctor said David's condition is still up in the air. We won't know more until he wakes up and they run more tests."

Lucas nodded gravely, his hand on Irene's shoulder for support. "Thanks for being here, Ryan. We really appreciate it."

"Can you two watch over him for now?"

"Yeah, we can handle it. You should also go check on Tyson," Lucas suggested.

With one last hug, Ryan said goodbye to the Millers. "Please keep me posted. Call if you need anything," he told them, locking eyes with Lucas, who nodded in agreement.

He needed some time to gather his thoughts, make a plan, and ensure that David got the justice and support he deserved.

Stepping out of the hospital, a whirlwind of emotions churned inside him. Seeing David lying there helpless in that hospital bed haunted his thoughts, and it fueled his determination to uncover the truth and make those responsible pay.

Ryan had decided to crash at David's place, mainly to keep an eye on Tyson and to ensure the house didn't feel so empty. It was a stark contrast to his own place up in Hackney, which suddenly felt as important as a forgotten sock.

But before he could settle in at David's, he had to deal with something essential: clothes. So, he hopped on the tube, zipping from Westminster to Hackney in a jiffy. After the train ride, he found himself not far from his own flat. A bit of fresh air and a short walk seemed like it could clear his head.

Ryan couldn't help but wish that what had happened was just a terrible nightmare. He wanted to wake up with Tyson snuggled beside him and the sound of David's laughter filling the air. But life was far from kind.

He turned towards his neighborhood, fondly nicknamed "Shady Street" by David. Despite its quirks, it was home. David had offered him a fancier place, but Ryan preferred the simplicity of his studio.

Once inside, he dumped his clothes on the sofa and took refuge in a hot shower. The water, like a comforting embrace, offered a brief escape from the chaos of recent events. As it washed over him, he contemplated the uncertain road ahead.

After the shower, he threw on some fresh clothes and started packing a bag with the essentials. In the midst of shuffling clothes around, his phone started ringing. He glanced at the caller ID and saw it was his girlfriend, Elle.

"Hey, Elle?" he answered, his voice carrying exhaustion.

"Ryan? Where have you been? I've been trying to reach you all night, and you've been ghosting me," Elle's tone revealed her frustration.

Ryan was in no mood for this. He had more pressing matters on his plate. "I was caught up," he sighed.

"Nice try, mister. I'm not falling for it."

"There was an emergency, alright? Look, I'm sorry, but I don't have the time for this right now. I'll catch you later," Ryan replied, not waiting for Elle's comeback before ending the call.

After finishing his packing, Ryan left his flat. He knew he needed some time off from work, so that was his next stop.

Ryan worked as a personal trainer at a gym. He still had some accrued time off that he hadn't used. Ryan wasn't the type to take breaks; he was always fully committed to his work.

He swiped his gym card at the entrance, and the door beeped open. Inside, he was greeted by Andy, one of his co-workers, who seemed overly enthusiastic.

"Ryan! Hey, mate, you okay?" Andy's energy was a bit much for Ryan that morning.

"Yeah, I'm fine. Is Craig around today?" Ryan wanted to avoid further questions about his well-being.

"He's in his office. Why?" Andy's curiosity seemed insatiable.

"I can't explain right now. Thanks, though." Ryan patted Andy on the back and made his way to Craig's office.

Entering the office, Ryan found his boss hunched over his desk, engrossed in paperwork. Craig was a compassionate man who also knew David. Ryan hoped he'd understand his need for time off.

Ryan knocked on the door, and Craig looked up as he entered.

"Hey, boss. Do you have a minute?" Ryan asked.

"Yeah, sure. Come in. Close the door, will you?" Craig motioned, and Ryan followed his instruction.

Ryan took a seat across from Craig. "Is it okay if I use up all my time off?"

Craig raised an eyebrow. "Why? What's going on? You never take time off."

With a sigh, Ryan decided to share the whole story with Craig. "It's about David. He was badly beaten and had to undergo surgery last night." Ryan's emotions started to overwhelm him again, but Craig got up from his desk and sat in front of him.

"Hey, hey. It's okay. We're here for you. Knowing David, he'll recover. He's a stubborn fool, after all," Craig reassured him.

"Thank you."

"Consider it granted. Let me know if we can visit David, and we'll support you, okay? You're not alone in this. David is loved," Craig said, and Ryan nodded, appreciating the kind words.

The only task he had for the day was to return to Knightsbridge and take care of David's house. A long time ago, David had given him a spare key. Whenever Ryan felt down, David had told him he could use the key to unwind. Despite having never used it before, this seemed like the perfect opportunity.

Upon entering David's flat, Tyson welcomed him.

"Sorry, Tyson. Your Dad won't be home for a while. But don't worry, little one, I am here," Ryan comforted Tyson, who responded with a lick.

After setting Tyson down, he went to the kitchen, fetched cat food, and filled Tyson's bowl. He patted the cat before entering David's room. It had been a while since he had been in his friend's room, so he took in the surroundings.

David's room was minimalist yet exuded class and modernity, almost as if David didn't sleep there.

While exploring the room, Ryan noticed a picture on a vanity table and examined it closely. The photo depicted him and David from the early days of their friendship, taken during a school trip to New York. Ryan recalled being unable to afford the trip, but David had saved enough money to make it possible for him to attend. Though they occasionally had disagreements, their conflicts never lasted long.

As he gazed at the photo, an idea emerged in Ryan's mind, and he began to formulate a plan.

5

David

H E COULD HEAR BEEPING NOISES, and he felt like he'd been dropped into a puzzling dream. He couldn't quite figure out where he was or who he was, and the voices chatting around him only added to the confusion. Blinking felt like trying to lift a heavy weight, and it was a struggle.

"Doctor, anything?" Someone asked, their voice strangely comforting in the midst of the chaos.

"His vital signs are looking up, but we'll need to run some brain scans to be sure."

"When can we move him to a regular room? David's parents want to pay a visit."

David. The name triggered something inside him, a flicker of recognition that he couldn't quite grasp. It felt like trying to catch smoke with his bare hands.

"We can probably shift him later today. He doesn't seem to be in any immediate danger, but we'll keep an eye on him."

"Thanks, doctor."

"You're welcome, Ryan."

Ryan, the name echoed in his mind. He found an odd sense of comfort in the warm tones of the mysterious man.

Eventually, David managed to open his eyes, only to find himself in a room engulfed in darkness. He figured the lights were probably off.

The room was decently sized, and the incessant beeping seemed to have subsided.

As he scanned the surroundings slowly, he noticed a man lying on a neatly made cot. David assumed the man was asleep, given the faint snores he could hear.

David wanted to strike up a conversation and grab the man's attention, but he soon realised his mouth was obstructed by some mouthpiece he hadn't noticed before.

The man stirred and blinked, locking eyes with David.

"D-David?" That voice was familiar, undoubtedly Ryan.

David wanted to smile but couldn't, so he settled for a nod.

"Are you feeling okay? Do you need anything? Wait here, let me call someone."

Ryan leaped into action, frantically tending to matters in the room they were in.

Moments later, the room became a whirlwind of activity, with nurses checking his eyes and everything else. David had no clue why he was in the hospital, but he figured he'd have to wait a bit longer to get that crucial detail.

He could still hear and feel Ryan's presence. Now, Ryan was engaged in a phone conversation.

"Yeah, he's awake… You can definitely visit. I forgot to tell you they took him out of the ICU moments ago. I guess I fell asleep. Okay… See you later," Ryan said, concluding his call.

David watched as Ryan turned his attention back to him, walking closer. He couldn't quite put his finger on it, but he felt an urge to reach out and offer reassurance to Ryan.

Just who are you, Ryan?

David's body felt incredibly heavy once again. He didn't want to fall asleep.

He didn't want to miss Ryan.

Ryan smiled softly at him. "I know you're tired. Go ahead and sleep some more. Your parents will be here when you wake up."

David tried to raise his hand to point at Ryan, managing to do so with difficulty, given the presence of the nurses around him. Ryan was patient, though, and seemed to understand what he wanted to say. "Me?" Ryan asked, and David attempted a curt nod. "I'll be here. I'm not going anywhere."

That was the last thing he heard before finally succumbing to sleep once more.

When he woke up again, he noticed that the room was a little brighter now.

David guessed it was finally morning. He looked around and saw Ryan and two other people talking to a man in a suit.

"In this moment, we haven't identified the man yet, but we do have CCTV footage of the incident. Unfortunately, it was quite dark, so it might take some time to track down the suspect,"

"That's the best we can hope for, isn't it, Detective?"

"Yes, Mr. Miller. We're just as eager to apprehend these individuals. This isn't the first time something like this has occurred," the Detective continued.

The older woman in the room, she couldn't help but cry, and it hit David hard. He just wanted to give her a hug.

The Detective let out a heavy sigh, "We suspect that these are the same individuals responsible for multiple similar crimes. Let's just say, David is fortunate to have survived." Ryan gave a nod and added, "I should head off now. Keep me updated."

The older woman leaned on Ryan for support, and David felt a pang of guilt. These were supposed to be his parents, but he couldn't even recognize them. It was like a punch in the gut.

They turned and caught him watching them. Ryan stepped in, "David, these two lovely people here are your parents, Irene and Lucas Miller." He said it kindly, confirming David's guess.

David managed a weak nod, feeling utterly helpless. He wished he could give them a reassuring smile or say something comforting, but the thing covering his mouth kept him quiet. Every second just added to his frustration, and he wanted it off.

Nothing was making sense, and he just wanted some answers.

David had loads of questions, but all he could do for now was sit tight and wonder.

"We're really sorry, love," David's Dad said, sounding genuinely regretful, though David couldn't quite figure out why they were apologizing.

His Mum reached out for his bandaged hand, and her touch brought a bit of comfort amid the chaos in his head. He felt grateful for that simple connection.

Looking back at Ryan, David felt a sense of peace in his eyes, like he understood and was willing to wait.

"The doc said they'll remove that mouthpiece later today," Ryan told David.

David's heart skipped a beat at the thought of getting his voice back, and he couldn't help but feel grateful. He found himself drawn to Ryan in a way he couldn't quite explain, a connection that stirred up emotions he was still trying to figure out.

All sorts of questions swirled in David's head as he grappled with these intense feelings for Ryan. Maybe he was attracted to men? The way he felt around him seemed to suggest it.

A little while later, the doctor finally walked in.

As the doctor gently took off the mouthpiece, David felt a rush of relief. Breathing in the cool, free air was a gift, and he savored it.

The doctor's voice was friendly and encouraging, urging David to take that first step. "Alright, that's off. Hopefully, you're feeling a bit better now without it. Can you try and talk to us for a bit?"

Fear gripped David, threatening to choke his words. He mustered every ounce of determination and managed to croak out a shaky, "H-Hello?" His voice was rough and strained.

David noticed Ryan's emotional reaction. He thought he saw a glint of tears in Ryan's eyes before he turned away. Whatever connection they had, it felt strong in that room.

His parents were a mix of sobs and smiles. Their tears seemed to be tears of joy, the kind you shed when you're incredibly relieved to see your son respond, even if just a little.

The offer of ice chips from the doctor was a godsend for David's parched throat. Ryan handed them over with care, and David savored the cool relief.

The doctor, all professional, kept asking questions. David could only manage simple "yes" or "no" answers because his voice was still weak.

"Do you remember who you are?" the doctor asked, gently but probing.

David hesitated, a strange feeling settling in as he tried to grasp his own identity. "N-no," he eventually admitted.

He felt the weight of his parents' disappointment and saw Ryan struggling to hold back his emotions.

"Do you remember these people with us right now?" the doctor pressed on, and David's heart sank as he spoke the truth.

"No," he replied, the word heavy on his tongue, acknowledging the vast gap separating him from these strangers who claimed to be his family and friend.

With one more question to go, David braced himself for another revelation. The doctor's next question dug deep, probing his very existence.

"Can you remember anything right now?" the doctor asked.

David shut his eyes tightly, as if trying to squeeze out elusive memories. But the emptiness remained, leaving him lost and disoriented.

The frustration and confusion gnawed at him.

"No," David admitted, and the doctor made some notes, his expression unreadable.

"Thank you, David," the doctor said kindly. "I'll be back tomorrow with my findings. For now, enjoy your time with your family."

The room felt heavy with questions, and David couldn't escape the weight of his own past hanging over him.

"Do you want to lay back down?" Ryan asked with a kind smile.

"Yeah, please," David replied.

Back in bed, surrounded by his parents and Ryan, David's curiosity got the better of him. "W-what happened?" His voice still sounded weak from everything he'd been through.

"I think we should wait for the doctor's verdict tomorrow. We promise to tell you what we know," his Mum said, cupping his face and planting a kiss on his cheek.

"You two should head back home. I'll take care of David," Ryan assured them.

"Are you sure? What about Tyson?" David's Mum asked.

David was juggling so many names all at once; it was starting to give him a headache.

"Don't worry about Tyson. He's currently with Layla, getting spoiled," Ryan chuckled, and David found comfort in that sound.

"Okay, call us if anything," his Dad said before kissing David's forehead.

Ryan escorted his parents out and returned to David's side.

"Tyson?" David asked Ryan.

"He's your cat. You spoil him rotten, and he's missing you right now," Ryan replied.

"I have a cat?" David asked, looking at Ryan's warm and inviting smile.

"Yeah, you two were inseparable. Your parents even call you two a troublemaking duo," Ryan said. "I actually have pictures of him and you together. Want to see?"

Ryan pulled out his phone and showed David a picture. It was a man wearing a checkered shirt and the tightest jeans known to humanity, and an orange cat sticking its tongue out.

"Is that me?" David asked Ryan.

"Yeah, that's you and Tyson when you adopted him from the rescue centre. You were over the moon because you'd wanted a cat for ages," Ryan explained.

"I… I can't remember any of it," David sighed and closed his eyes.

"Don't worry. We'll help you remember," Ryan reassured him, giving his hand a gentle squeeze.

David turned his head to face Ryan. "What are we to each other? Are you my brother?" he asked, earning a hearty chuckle.

"No, not brothers, although we act like it sometimes. We're best friends, David. You're one of the most important people in my life," Ryan said sincerely.

David didn't know what to say, so he went with the next question on his mind. "Was I gay?" Ryan burst into laughter.

"What's so funny?" David couldn't help but smile, even though it hurt a bit.

"Nothing. It's just that you couldn't be straight if you tried, and I wouldn't have it any other way," Ryan said.

David managed to chuckle but soon grew serious again. "I'm sorry."

"For what?" Ryan asked, his worry evident.

"For forgetting us…" David managed to say before sleep overcame him.

He could feel Ryan brushing his hair off his forehead, and he smiled.

6

David

DAVID SAT UP IN BED, his eyes fixed on the doctor doing his usual checkup.

David's parents had come over in the morning, bringing breakfast that smelled amazing. But they were holding off on giving him real food until they got the medical go-ahead.

The doctor glanced between David's parents and David himself, looking composed but with a touch of seriousness. "I've got some good news and some not-so-good news," he began, making everyone hold their breath.

David watched as the doctor delivered the good news, a glimmer of hope washing over the room. "The good news is that the brain swelling in David has started to go down," the doctor confirmed.

"And the bad news?" His Dad asked.

"The not-so-good news is that, as I told Ryan earlier, because of the serious brain injury and trauma David went through, we believe he's got something called Dissociative Amnesia," the doctor explained gently.

The words hung heavy in the air, and the room felt like it was holding its breath. David's eyes darted between his worried parents and Ryan.

Summoning his courage, David asked the doctor, his voice shaky, "What does that mean?"

The doctor kept a kind gaze on David as he began to explain Dissociative Amnesia. "Dissociative Amnesia," he started, picking his words carefully, "happens when the brain experiences severe trauma." His eyes showed understanding as he went on, "In your case, David, it's probably a response to the tough things you've been through. It's a kind of memory loss where you might have gaps in your memory."

David frowned as he tried to take it all in.

The doctor continued, giving more details. "These gaps can cover different parts of your life, from personal memories to even your own identity. It's like some parts of your life story are temporarily hidden from your conscious mind."

David's parents and Ryan listened closely, their faces showing concern and support. The room held a feeling of empathy and shared worry.

The doctor finished, "With time, therapy, and a supportive environment, many folks with Dissociative Amnesia can slowly get their lost memories back. It's a journey, David."

David, with a mix of curiosity and apprehension in his voice, asked, "How long will it take for me to remember everything?"

The doctor, patient as ever, replied, "The thing is, this type of amnesia varies from person to person. It could take days, months, or even years."

David nodded, even though the uncertainty was eating at him.

"Will I be able to leave the hospital soon?"

"I'm afraid we'll need to keep you here for a few more days before I can let you go," the doctor said.

The thought of staying in the hospital for a long time didn't sit well with David, but he knew it was needed.

"Don't worry, doc. We've got him covered," Ryan said, sounding determined. David's parents nodded in agreement, their faces showing both worry and relief.

"Alright then. It looks like you've got a solid support team here. I'll head out," the doctor said, excusing himself.

Once they were alone, David couldn't hold back his pressing question. "Can you finally tell me what happened?"

Ryan moved closer, taking a seat by David's bedside. "You went on a date that night. I kept bugging you about it because I was concerned. You left me in charge of Tyson, but when I didn't hear from you, I started to get really worried. Then, that's when I got the call," Ryan's voice quivered, and tears welled up in his eyes. David reached out and gave Ryan's hand a gentle squeeze, a silent way of offering comfort and understanding.

"We were terrified, David. Terrified that we might lose you. And I... we couldn't bear that. We couldn't lose you," Ryan confessed.

David held Ryan's hand and gave it a firm grip. "You couldn't have known. And it sounds like it was my fault," David admitted, his voice heavy with emotion. He glanced around the room at his parents and Ryan. "I'm sorry for scaring all of you. I may not remember everything, but right now, I really appreciate all of you being there for me."

Tears rolled down David's cheeks as he let go of the guilt and fear that had been weighing on him.

Finally, the day came when the doctor returned to discharge him. David felt a wave of relief as he listened to the doctor's instructions about keeping the bandage on for a few more days and keeping it dry. He nodded, eager to do whatever it took to leave the hospital.

However, he was annoyed when they insisted on wheeling him out in a wheelchair. David grumbled about it, but it seemed like standard procedure, so he reluctantly accepted it.

As they left the hospital, David turned to Ryan, who was pushing his wheelchair. "Where are we heading?"

"We're going to your place in Knightsbridge. I hope you don't mind me staying there while you were in the hospital."

"That's okay. I didn't even know I had my own house," David admitted with a wry smile, adding a touch of self-deprecating humor to his words.

Just then, his Dad impatiently honked the car's horn, signaling that their ride had arrived.

With the help of Ryan and his Dad, David was carefully transferred into the car, taking the passenger seat. Ryan returned the wheelchair to the hospital before joining them in the vehicle.

Driving away from the hospital, David couldn't help but feel grateful and relieved. He might not remember much about his life, but he knew having folks like Ryan and his family around was something special.

They finally got to his flat, much later than expected. London traffic was every bit as notorious as its reputation, making the journey feel like a never-ending puzzle.

David's parents kindly offered to come up to his flat with him, but he declined politely. They'd done plenty already, and he didn't want to take up more of their time. They seemed relieved to see him in his own place, trusting Ryan to look after him.

Stepping into his supposed home, David felt a strange mix of familiarity and strangeness. He couldn't remember this place, but it was supposed to be his home.

As soon as Ryan opened the door, a friendly feline voice greeted them.

They both looked down to see an orange cat purring happily as it circled around David's legs. David crouched down carefully, not wanting to strain himself, and picked up the friendly kitty.

"You must be Tyson. You're a cute one, aren't you?" David cooed to the cat, his voice filled with genuine affection.

"Meow," Tyson replied, as if confirming his name, and Ryan chuckled warmly beside him.

"I thought he was with Layla?" David asked Ryan, genuinely curious about this Layla person.

"I asked her to bring him here while you were asleep last night. Don't worry; I came back as soon as Tyson was home."

"Is she your girlfriend?"

Ryan chuckled at the question. "No, not at all. She's a friend. You two were friends first, and then you introduced us. That's a story for another time."

David went along with the explanation for now, thinking there would be plenty of time to unravel these mysteries later. "Alright, let's get you settled so I can whip up some dinner," Ryan suggested, taking charge of the situation.

David gently placed Tyson on the floor, and together, they ventured further into his house.

David's place was a burst of color and personality, and he couldn't help but be charmed by it. Every corner held a new detail, a unique piece of decor, and he soaked it all in with delight.

"Is this really my place? This is incredible," David marveled, unable to contain his awe.

Ryan chuckled softly from behind him, his voice brimming with affection. "Yeah, you were quite specific when you designed this place; you nearly drove your interior designer up the wall."

David couldn't help but laugh at the thought. "I can only imagine; it's a lot, but in a good way."

Ryan's hand gently landed on David's shoulder, radiating warmth and comfort. "How about you settle in the living room while I get dinner going?" he suggested.

David took the suggestion to heart, making his way to the living room and finding a cozy spot to relax in. Tyson hopped onto his lap, and David started stroking the cat's soft fur.

As he leaned back in the comfortable chair, the day's events finally caught up with him, and David felt a wave of exhaustion wash over him. Tyson's rhythmic purring filled the room, creating a soothing tune that relaxed his tense muscles and eased his worried mind.

Closing his eyes, he let himself unwind for the first time in what felt like ages. The last thing he heard before drifting into a well-deserved nap was the comforting sound of Tyson's purring.

7

Ryan

"DAVID DINNER'S READY," Ryan called out.

Ryan felt relieved that David was going to be alright, memory loss or not. What mattered was that David was alive and with him. Still, he couldn't shake off the worry that whoever had attacked David might still be out there, a potential threat.

"Not on my watch," Ryan muttered to himself.

Ryan hadn't cooked in David's kitchen before because he didn't want to make a mess of things. He was a decent cook, planning his own meals as a personal trainer and to save money. But cooking for David felt different.

When Ryan didn't get a response, he hurried to the living room, thinking something might have happened.

To his surprise, he found David lightly snoring with Tyson in his lap, and it brought a chuckle to Ryan's lips. It almost felt like nothing had ever happened.

Grabbing a blanket from the couch, Ryan covered David gently. He carefully lifted Tyson off David's lap to tuck him in properly. David looked so peaceful, and while part of him wanted to watch his friend sleep, he knew that would be a bit creepy, so he decided against it.

After making sure David was tucked in, Ryan returned to the kitchen to safely store the food he had prepared when he heard his phone ringing. He quickly took out his phone from his pocket to check, and it was Elle calling. She had been ringing him incessantly during his time at the hospital with David, and he had been sending her straight to voicemail each time.

He knew it wasn't exactly what a good boyfriend should do, but his priority at that moment was David.

Ryan let out a sigh and answered the call. "Elle."

"Don't 'Elle' me, you idiot. You've been dodging my calls for the past couple of days, and that's all you have to say?" Elle's voice was filled with anger.

"Look, Elle. I'm sorry, okay? I already told you there was an emergency, and I couldn't answer your calls," Ryan said wearily. He really didn't have the energy for this right now.

"What kind of emergency makes you completely cut me off? Are you cheating on me? Who's the other woman?" Elle's voice was getting louder and more frantic.

"Will you please lower your voice, Elle? You're starting to sound unhinged. No, there's no one else. If you're this suspicious, maybe we should just end this now," Ryan said firmly.

"No! I'm sorry, alright. I don't know what got into me," Elle replied, her tone softening.

"Goodnight, Elle. I'm tired and just want to rest, okay? We'll talk soon," Ryan said before ending the call without waiting for Elle's response.

Then he thought of David, his David. The only person who accepted him for every single flaw he had without judgment. What he had told David before the attack still stood. If he was gay, he would never let David go.

He closed his eyes, and suddenly, his thoughts drifted to David's lips and hands. He opened his eyes instantly, not knowing where those thoughts had come from.

What the hell?

"Ryan?" Ryan's head shot up as soon as he heard David's voice from the kitchen doorway, and now Ryan couldn't stop looking at David's lips. He shook it off; he was probably just tired and seeing things. "Who were you talking to?" David continued.

"It's no one," Ryan cleared his throat, which had suddenly gone dry. "Are you hungry? I made some food for us."

David nodded, and he couldn't help but feel that this wasn't his old friend. They were in the same body, but at the same time, they both acted differently. This version of David was more subdued and reserved compared to his old self. Ryan promised himself that he would get his friend back, and he wouldn't back down on it.

"You can cook?" David asked, and Ryan thought he looked cute with his head tilted to the side.

Stop it, Ryan. Not the time to be thinking of David like that.

"Yeah, but not as good as you, though. Come on in, I made some of your favourite chicken pasta," Ryan said and helped David into the kitchen, where they both sat down.

"I can cook?"

"Oh yes! You were the better cook out of the two of us. You helped me learn how to cook, actually, and you were very patient with me."

He remembered those days when David taught him how to cook. He kept burning the food, but David just stood there, being his understanding self. Ryan had never heard David yell at him for messing up.

"You shouldn't be too hard on yourself because this is incredible, Ryan."

Ryan felt his cheeks getting hot from the compliment.

"I had a pretty good teacher, I suppose."

He saw David eat his food with gusto, and Ryan was thrilled that his friend had gotten his appetite back.

"Sorry, I was hungrier than I thought," David said, suddenly looking incredibly shy.

Ryan chuckled at his friend. "Don't worry about it. I'll cook some more for you tomorrow if you want."

"Really? You'd do that?"

"Of course. Anything for you," Ryan said, and he meant it.

"Thank you," David said and placed his hand on the table and Ryan held it without thinking.

"Come on, let's get you to your room so you can rest."

David nodded. "Can I shower first? I am pretty sure I stink of the hospital by now."

Ryan chuckled. "Okay, I'll wait by your bed and take some clothes out for you."

"You don't have to do that."

"I want to. It's the least I can do."

David looked like he wanted to say something but stopped himself halfway through and just nodded.

Ryan guided David to his room and led him to the bathroom.

He headed straight to David's closet, and once he opened it, he found it incredibly organized by colour. Ryan didn't know about this, so he learned something new today about his friend.

He took out some clothes that he thought seemed fitting to sleep in and placed them on David's bed.

He sat down on the edge of the bed and waited for David to finish taking a bath. David wanted to shower, but Ryan had reminded him that he couldn't get his head bandage wet, so he relented for a bath.

After a while of waiting, David finally came out, with only a towel covering him, and his chest exposed. Ryan could see the damage that had been done to his friend, which made him furious, but he also saw how fit his friend looked. He had never really noticed it before, but David was well-built underneath all the layers of clothing he usually wore.

His thoughts wandered to his tongue, licking all the droplets of water on David's body, which made his trousers tighter than normal.

Bloody hell, what's happening to me?

He shook off the thoughts and thought of his grandparents to keep the swelling in his trousers down.

"Ryan?" David said, and Ryan saw that David was trying to hide his body from him, and he understood.

David didn't want Ryan to see him that way. The look of uncertainty and doubt crossed David's features, and it nearly broke him.

"Uh, yes. Your clothes are here," Ryan said, standing up. "Are you going to be okay?"

"Y-yes. Thank you," David replied, looking him in the eye.

Ryan got lost in his gaze before clearing his throat.

"Right, I'll be right out on the couch if you need me," Ryan said, and David nodded.

He left David's room and took a deep breath. He honestly didn't know what was happening to him. He had never seen his friend this way before. He didn't want to think any further and just headed to the couch and prepared to sleep.

This has been the strangest day.

8

Ryan

RYAN WOKE UP EARLY, feeling the need to attend to Tyson, who was already complaining that none of his humans were awake to cater to his royal highness. After feeding the feline royalty, he decided to take a quick shower before preparing breakfast for both himself and David.

While in the midst of cooking David's favorite Full English Breakfast, his phone rang. Glancing at the caller ID, he initially thought it was Elle, but it turned out to be David's Mum, Irene.

"Good morning, Irene," Ryan greeted warmly, always enjoying conversations with David's parents as if they were his own.

"How are you and David doing?" Irene inquired, her tone reflecting some relief now that David was back home.

"We're doing okay. David is still asleep, and I'm cooking us breakfast."

"That's good. Listen, I want you guys to visit here. Maybe it will trigger some memories for David."

"We could, but I don't think we should push David like that, Irene. It might overwhelm him," Ryan responded, expressing his concerns.

"I understand. I just… never mind. Please come and visit anyway. Lucas has been baking cookies non-stop since we got home yesterday."

"Of course, we'll be there before lunch. Talk to you soon," Ryan agreed before ending the call after exchanging pleasantries.

Ryan finished cooking and was suddenly enveloped in a warm hug from behind. It took him by surprise, but he couldn't help but smile, recognizing that this was a different side of David. The embrace felt oddly right, though Ryan couldn't quite put his finger on why.

Turning around, he met David, dressed in just a bathrobe and a pair of pants. Ryan's trousers seemed to have a mind of their own, growing tighter at the sight. He couldn't understand why he was feeling this way; he had always considered himself straight and had never questioned it before.

David cocked his head, breaking the moment. "Ryan, are we going to eat, or are we just going to stand here and stare at each other?"

Get it together, Ryan.

"Uh, yeah. I made us some breakfast," Ryan finally managed to respond.

David chuckled. "Yeah, I could see and smell that. This looks great; can't wait to taste it."

"Well, let's have a morning feast then, shall we?" Ryan suggested, offering a warm smile to David.

David gave him another hug, and this time, Ryan hugged his friend back, relishing in his comforting presence.

As they broke apart and settled down to eat, Tyson joined them, hopping onto David's lap and purring contentedly.

Ryan took in the scene before him, silently wishing that they could stay in this moment forever.

They tucked into their breakfast, savoring the meal in a comfortable silence. Ryan couldn't help but notice the little sounds of satisfaction David made as he ate, which stirred something within him. It was a confusing feeling, one he couldn't quite put his finger on, but he brushed it aside for now.

David's voice broke the silence. "So, what are we doing today?"

"Your parents want us to visit them today, and I told them to expect us just before lunch," Ryan replied, trying to keep the mood positive.

David seemed to ponder that for a moment before letting out a sigh. "Where do they live?"

Ryan couldn't ignore the frustration and sadness in David's voice. He leaned in, offering support. "Hey, don't worry about not remembering, okay?"

"I know," David replied with a hint of resignation. "It just sucks that I can't even remember my own parents, let alone where they lived."

Ryan could sense the frustration in his friend, and he empathized deeply. "You know what, once we finish breakfast, I'll take you to our favorite hangout spot. How does that sound?"

David nodded, a small smile forming on his face. It seemed like Ryan's offer had lightened his mood, even if just a little.

After getting ready for their day out, Ryan contemplated taking the tube, but a quick glance at David made him reconsider. The London Underground might not be the most comfortable choice for David right now, so they opted for an Uber.

Ryan booked their Uber, and he couldn't help but smile at David's excitement. David was captivated by a street performer nearby, his face filled with genuine curiosity. It was reassuring to see that this part of David's personality remained unchanged despite his amnesia.

Their Uber arrived, and Ryan opened the door for David. David, still buzzing with curiosity, couldn't resist asking, "Where are you taking me?"

Ryan chuckled. "Well, it wouldn't be a surprise if I told you, would it?"

David playfully pouted. "You're such an arse."

"Oh, come on," Ryan teased, "I did cook for you this morning, and I get this treatment? Totally not fair, mate."

David smacked Ryan on the arm, and they both shared a laugh, relishing this simple, joyful moment reminiscent of their old times.

They arrived at Hyde Park shortly afterward. Stepping out of the Uber, Ryan watched as David's eyes widened in amazement.

"Where are we?" David asked, wonder in his voice.

"We're in Hyde Park," Ryan replied softly. "It's one of the places we like to go when we just want to be."

David turned to him, a smile tugging at his lips, though unshed tears glistened in his eyes. Ryan tenderly wiped them away.

"I'm sorry," David began, "I'm sorry for losing everything. I'm sure we had fun here together, and I just…"

Ryan continued to cup David's cheek, finding comfort in the warmth of his touch. "What did I tell you this morning? No more apologizing. What happened to you wasn't your fault, okay?"

David nodded and then pulled Ryan into a hug. Ryan cherished the embrace, feeling the connection they shared.

"Come on," Ryan said as they broke apart, "let's head inside."

Hyde Park in the summer held a special charm, and as Ryan strolled its sun-drenched trails with David by his side, he couldn't help but smile.

"You know, this place is our little slice of paradise," Ryan said, glancing at his friend.

David, taking in the vibrant scenery, nodded in agreement.

They passed a group of kids splashing in the Serpentine Lake, their laughter filling the air like a joyful melody.

"What's your favourite memory here?" David asked, curiosity in his voice.

Ryan's smile broadened. "Well, one of my favorites is when we tried paddle boating on the lake."

David furrowed his brow. "We did?"

"Yeah," Ryan replied, "it was a total disaster. We couldn't steer the darn thing to save our lives."

David laughed, the sound soothing to Ryan's soul. "Sounds like something we'd do."

They found a secluded spot by the lake, where the water sparkled with the reflection of the clear blue sky. Ryan pointed to a nearby tree.

"That's our thinking tree, Dave," he said, a touch of nostalgia in his voice.

David furrowed his brow. "Thinking tree?"

"Yeah," Ryan explained. "Whenever one of us had a problem or needed to clear our heads, we'd sit under that tree and talk it out. It's seen its fair share of our secrets."

David gave a small smile. "It must be a wise old tree."

As they settled beneath the shade of their "thinking tree," Ryan continued to share stories, each anecdote infused with the warmth of their friendship.

"Remember the ice cream truck that used to come here every weekend?" Ryan asked, a playful gleam in his eye.

David's eyes lit up with curiosity. "Oh, yeah?"

Ryan nodded. "And we'd try a different flavor each time."

David grinned. "Did I have a favorite?"

"You were all about that mint chocolate chip," Ryan said, his tone filled with affection.

They talked and laughed, with Ryan offering glimpses into their shared past. Even though David couldn't remember, their connection remained strong, anchored in the simple pleasures of their friendship and the beauty of Hyde Park in the summer.

As they left Hyde Park and booked another Uber to get to West Ealing for a visit to David's folks, David couldn't help but ask, "So, my parents live in one of the poshest areas in West London?"

Ryan chuckled softly, "You could say that. At first, they weren't too keen on living in such a fancy place."

Curiosity piqued, David asked, "What changed their minds?"

Ryan replied with a warm smile, "You did."

"Me?"

"Yeah, you. Once your career took off, you thought it'd be nice to give them a bit of peace and quiet. So, you convinced them to move to their current place, and you even footed the bill."

David looked a bit surprised, "I did? What was I doing for a living?"

"You were a stylist for celebs," Ryan answered, a touch of nostalgia in his voice. He couldn't help but notice David's lips, which distracted him for a moment. Clearing his throat, he continued, "None of the folks you worked with knew what happened, not yet anyway. But don't worry, I'll handle it." Ryan chuckled, knowing he'd have to deal with David's agent, who was always a handful. "We'll figure it out."

David reached out and placed his hand on Ryan's lap, sending a rush of warmth and discomfort through Ryan. It was getting a bit too close for comfort, and he struggled to keep his composure. "Thanks," David said sincerely. "I don't think I'd be here without you."

Ryan put his hand on top of David's and gave him a reassuring smile. "You're welcome, David. We're in this together, remember?" Their bond was undeniable, and Ryan was determined to help his friend regain his memories and rebuild their lives.

9

Ryan

"DAVID, RYAN, COME ON IN," Irene greeted them with a big smile as she opened the door.

Ryan noticed Irene seemed in better spirits. The worry that had clouded her eyes before had vanished, and he genuinely felt happy about her improved mood.

On the other hand, David seemed a tad uneasy about seeing his parents again. Irene didn't mention it and just hugged them warmly.

"Hi, Irene," Ryan said as they pulled away. "Where's Lucas?"

"He's out back, grilling some steaks."

"Hi, Mum," David's voice quivered slightly.

"Your Dad's whipped up your favourite cookies, and they're already on the table."

As they headed inside, the delightful smell of white chocolate chip cookies, baked by David's Dad, wafted through the air. The scent always brought a smile to Ryan's face, conjuring memories of their shared moments over the years.

Seated at the dining table, Ryan sneakily reached for a cookie, but David slapped his hand away.

"Ow," Ryan pretended, blowing on his hand as if it really hurt.

"Ry! Where are your manners?" David scolded, and Ryan froze.

"You remember?" Ryan asked once he regained his composure.

"Remember what?" David looked confused.

"N-Nothing. Don't mind me."

"No, you can't escape now, Ryan Jameson Milton!" David declared, and Ryan couldn't help but laugh.

"Milton? Where did you even get that?" Ryan chuckled when David playfully smacked his shoulder.

"Well, you never told me your last name, did you?" David said, and it felt just like the old days between them.

"Alright, alright. Quit hitting me. My last name's Evans. Ryan Evans. No middle name, no fancy stuff."

"Well, Mr. Evans, someone needs to brush up on their table manners," David teased, shooting him a playful glare.

"Fine," Ryan conceded, glancing up to see Irene grinning at them. "Mrs. Miller, may I please have a cookie?"

"Well, Ryan, yes you may," Irene granted.

"See, Mr. Miller? Are you happy now?" Ryan quipped.

"Mhmm," David replied, grabbing his own cookie from the bowl.

"Where are your manners?" Ryan Mumbled softly, but he couldn't help but smile.

"What was that? Sorry, I was too busy enjoying this fab cookie. No wonder it was my fave," David moaned, and Ryan was relieved there was no alcohol involved, or it could have been a situation.

"Thanks, Mum," David added.

"You're welcome, sweetie," Irene said before pausing. "How's your head holding up? That bandage must feel a bit uncomfortable."

"It's alright, just a little headache here and there. But it's quite the fashion statement," David teased. Ryan made a mental note about the headaches, though, a tad concerned.

"That's good. Why don't you go join your Dad in the garden while he's grilling?" Irene suggested to David.

David looked at Ryan, almost seeking permission.

"Go on. I'll be fine in here with your Mum. Join your Dad," Ryan assured him, and David nodded.

David took another cookie and left Ryan with Irene.

Ryan got up and joined Irene in washing the dishes, stealing glances at David and Lucas in the garden through the kitchen window.

Irene turned to him and asked, "How are you holding up, Ryan?"

He paused from his dishwashing. "Could be better, to be honest. But I guess that's par for the course after everything that's gone down."

Irene smiled warmly at him. "I just want to say thank you for being there for him. We would've been in a right mess without you."

Ryan set down a dish and hugged Irene tightly. "No need for thanks. David's family, and so are you."

They broke the hug, and Irene suggested, "While they're out there, why don't you go up to David's room and see if you can find anything that might help him remember some stuff?"

Ryan liked the idea. "Alright, keep them occupied for a bit, yeah?" He flashed a smile, and Irene nodded.

Upstairs, David had ensured there was a spare room for himself when he bought this place for his parents. His room was a blast from his teenage past, an exact replica. His parents went along with it, just wanting him to be happy.

Ryan entered the second-story room, which was immaculate. He noticed pictures on the walls – shots of the two of them and some with David's parents.

He ventured further in and picked up a box tucked in the corner, filling it with items he thought might jog David's memory – photo albums, keepsakes, things he'd given David over the years. As he searched, he accidentally stepped on something beneath David's bed.

Curiosity piqued, he put his box down and crouched to find a hidden box. Sitting on David's bed, Ryan opened it and found letters, most dating back to their teenage years. He checked the addressee.

They were addressed to him. Every single one.

Ryan's hands shook as he decided to open the earliest letter he could find – one from fifteen years ago.

Dear Ryan,

I trust you're well, mate? It's only been a month since we started hanging out, but it feels like a proper age, doesn't it?

I've been doing some thinking, and I reckon I ought to let you in on something. There's no easy way to say this, but you're different, in the best way possible. Whenever I'm with you, it's like my day gets a bit brighter, and I can't help but smile.

Thing is, mate, my feelings have gone a bit wonky. I find myself feeling more than just mateship when I'm around you. It's all a bit baffling and a bit thrilling, to be honest.

I hope this doesn't sound too daft, and I'm not looking to mess up what we've got as mates. But I believe in being honest, and you mean a lot to me. No matter how this turns out – whether we stay the best of mates or things take a different turn – I want you to know that you're a big part of my life.

No matter what.

Cheers for being an amazing mate, Ryan.

Take care,

David

Ryan finished reading the first letter, his eyes getting all teary and his heart all mushy with memories. He couldn't help those tears threatening to spill and making the words on the page go all blurry. So, he carefully tucked the letter back into its envelope, his fingers shaking a bit as he sealed that piece of the past.

He took a deep breath, trying to steady himself, and then reached for another envelope, one that was just five months down the line from that first letter.

Dear Ryan,

I hope this letter finds you in good spirits. It's been a solid six months since we became mates, and I felt it's high time I dropped you a line.

So, mate, these past few months have been quite the journey. We've shared laughs, late-night talks, and even the odd adventure. It's been brilliant, and I'm grateful for every moment.

Here's the thing, though. I've been doing some soul-searching, and I've got to be honest with you. Those feelings I mentioned six months back, well, they haven't gone anywhere. In fact, they've only grown stronger.

I find myself thinking about you even when we're not together, and it's more than just friendship, mate. I'm still trying to figure it all out, and it's a bit daunting, to be honest.

I hope this doesn't throw a spanner in the works or make things weird between us. I value our friendship more than anything, and I don't want to mess that up.

No matter what.

All the best,

David

Ryan gently set the letter down, feeling a swirl of emotions bubbling up inside him. Curiosity, sadness, and a deep appreciation for this unexpected peek into their shared past.

"Why did you keep all this from me, David?" he whispered.

Unable to read any more letters at the moment, Ryan carefully gathered them all and placed them back in the box.

Just as he was about to close it, a soft knock on the door broke his thoughts.

"Ry, are you there? Mum said to come and get you," David's voice came from the other side.

"Yeah, I'll be out in a sec," Ryan replied, quickly organizing everything in the box and tying it up with a piece of string.

The door swung open, revealing David, his concern written all over his face. "Are you alright, Ryan?"

"Yeah, I'm fine," Ryan said, pushing his emotions aside. "Just got a bit sentimental, that's all."

David sat down next to him, glancing around the room. "Sentimental? About what?"

Ryan decided to lighten the mood. "About this room, mate. You do realize we're in your room, right?"

David looked at the pictures on the wall, considering. "Yeah, I can see that. Did we have a lot of good times here together?"

Ryan looked at David, and something inside him shifted. Those letters had stirred something he hadn't known was there.

"Ryan?" David's voice brought him back to the present as David took his hand.

"Y-Yeah," Ryan stammered, his heart racing. "You could say that. I'll tell you more about it when I'm ready. But for now, let's focus on the present," he said, giving David's hand a reassuring squeeze. Holding David's hand felt like coming home.

David changed the subject. "Well, we better get out of here then. The steaks are ready."

Ryan held onto David's hand and led him out of the room, the box of letters in his other hand. As they approached the door, David couldn't resist asking, "What's the box for?"

Ryan grinned, a warm excitement filling the air. "It's a surprise for later," he said, winking at David, conveying a heartfelt promise of something special in a casual tone.

Back with the Millers, they enjoyed a delicious dinner of grilled steaks, laughter, and stories, creating a cozy, relaxed atmosphere.

"Ryan, did I ever tell you about the time David tried to cook a steak for the first time and set the kitchen on fire?" Irene chuckled, sharing a fond look with David.

David frowned slightly, his voice tinged with sadness. "I wish I could remember that."

Ryan sympathized but didn't dwell on it, exchanging a knowing look with Irene and Lucas as they reminisced about their teenage years.

Feeling David's tiredness, Ryan decided it was time to call it a night. "Ready to head home?" he asked.

David gave him a weary smile. "Yeah, I think I've had my fill."

They said their goodbyes to David's parents, called for another Uber, and the ride home was uneventful.

Once back in the flat, David turned to Ryan. "You doing alright?" he asked.

"Yeah, mate, just wanted to say thanks for today. I appreciate what you did," David expressed his gratitude.

"No worries, buddy. Anything for my best mate," Ryan replied, grinning.

David nodded and their eyes met for a moment. Then, David leaned in and planted a friendly kiss on Ryan's cheek. "Goodnight, Ryan," he said before heading to his room.

Ryan touched his cheek, smiling at the warm sensation left by David's lips. He lingered for a moment, lost in the feeling, until Tyson's insistent meowing snapped him back to reality.

"Alright, Tyson, let's get you fed," Ryan told his demanding cat.

After tending to Tyson's hunger, he settled on the couch and placed the box he'd been holding on the coffee table. With a sense of curiosity, he decided to read just one more letter before turning in for the night.

Dear Ryan,

I wanted to follow up on what I shared with you a year ago. You've been nothing but supportive and understanding about my feelings, and I truly appreciate that. Since then, our friendship has meant even more to me.

These past five months have been a journey of self-discovery and understanding. I've come to terms with who I am, and I want you to know that I'm proud of it.

However, I also understand that you may not share those same feelings, and that's absolutely okay. What's most important to me is that we continue to cherish our friendship, our adventures, and the laughter we share.

Ryan, you've been an essential part of my life, and I'm thankful for your unwavering support. I'm content with whatever path our friendship takes.

No matter what.

Take care, my friend.

Sincerely,

David

10

David

"PLEASE DON'T..." *David heard himself say but it sounded like as if he was underwater.*

"Shut up. Your kind don't belong here." There was a man in front of him. He couldn't see the man's face because everything was dark.

The next thing he knew, he was on the floor and that everything hurt.

"David? David, wake up," Ryan's voice, familiar and comforting, pulled David from his nightmare.

He jolted awake, breathing heavily, finding solace in Ryan's presence beside him. Clinging to his friend, David tried not to let the tears well up. "R-Ryan?"

Ryan's hand caressed his shoulder, soothing. "Shh, you're okay. You're with me. No one's going to harm you." And David believed it, right down to his core.

They held onto each other for a while, and David cherished the warmth and safety he felt when he was in Ryan's arms.

Ryan's soft voice broke the silence. "Ready to talk about it?"

David shook his head, burying himself even closer to the man. Ryan always smelled amazing to him. "Not much to tell. Just a bad dream."

Though it felt all too real.

"Do you think it's a memory?" Ryan asked gently.

David pondered Ryan's words. "It could be, but I don't want to dwell on it right now." He really didn't. Whatever that dream was, it wasn't pleasant.

Ryan nodded in understanding. "I've got some good news for you today."

David looked up at Ryan, curious. "Yeah?"

Ryan cupped his face, brushing away unshed tears. "Yeah. The doc called this morning. He said he could check your bandage today and see if it's time to take it off."

David was relieved; it had been a whole week since he returned home, and the bandage on his head was getting on his nerves.

"So, when do we head to the doctor?"

Ryan chuckled. "No rush, mate. I've whipped up some breakfast. Fancy eating it in bed?"

David thought about it. "What about you?"

Ryan grinned. "I'll join you, and hey, I can finally reveal one of the things from that box."

David was curious about the box. He reckoned it was Ryan's way of helping him piece together his memories, and he was grateful for that.

Ryan returned with their food, and the aroma was incredible. Ryan admitted he wasn't much of a chef, but David thought he just needed more faith in his culinary skills.

Ryan settled next to David, and David wondered how they both fit in the same bed. Ryan was a big guy, but at the same time, David couldn't deny how snug and perfect their bodies seemed to fit together.

They ate in contented silence, savoring the delicious food. Afterward, they cuddled for a bit before Ryan got up to tidy away the dishes.

Are we this close before?

The thought weighed on David's heart and mind. Ryan felt so

familiar, yet David couldn't shake the feeling that they were somehow on different wavelengths. He pushed those thoughts aside and decided it was time to lend a hand.

Ryan had already done so much for him, and it was only fair to pull his own weight. David threw on a jacket, feeling a chill even in the summer heat. He wandered around the house and spotted Ryan crouched on the floor, petting Tyson.

David paused and watched the scene unfold, a warm feeling washing over him. It felt like Ryan belonged right here, in his house.

It suddenly struck David that he'd never asked where Ryan lived. He felt like he was doing a rubbish job at getting to know his supposed best friend, and he needed to change that.

"He's a cute one, isn't he?" David said as he strolled over to the two of them.

Ryan looked up and shot him a warm smile. Ryan's smile felt like a guiding light for those who were lost.

When did I start getting all poetic?

"Yeah, he's a real charmer," Ryan replied, looking back down at Tyson. "Go on, Tyson, go to your Dad."

"Meow," Tyson chimed in before giving Ryan's leg a good sniff and then making his way over to David.

David crouched down, extending his hand for Tyson to check out. Tyson took his sweet time with the sniffing ritual before nuzzling David's arm.

"I reckon he wants you to pick him up and give him some attention. Ain't that right, Tyson?"

"Meow," Tyson seemed to agree.

David chuckled at their little cat-chat before gently scooping Tyson up, cradling him like a baby.

"You're a chatty one, aren't you?" David whispered to Tyson, feeling his cat purr up a storm.

"Alright, let's take this to the living room. I've got something to show you," Ryan suggested.

David nodded and followed Ryan to the living room, with Tyson in tow. Ryan was already seated, and David took a spot next to him, sharing smiles. He placed Tyson on his lap, and the cat resumed his contented purring.

"So, what's this thing you wanted to show me?"

Ryan opened his hand, revealing a silver ring. "Well, it's not anything huge, but it's special to us."

"A ring?" David raised an eyebrow.

"Yeah, I found it in your room yesterday while I was looking for things that might jog your memory," Ryan explained, pausing for a moment as he looked at David. "It's the ring we gave each other as a promise that no matter what, we'd always be there for each other."

Ryan slid the ring onto David's ring finger, and it fit perfectly. "I never saw you wearing a ring. Why wasn't I wearing it all the time?"

"You were worried about losing it, so you kept it in your old room," Ryan clarified. He then reached under his shirt and pulled out a necklace that David hadn't noticed before. Now that he had, he couldn't help but keep his gaze on Ryan's chest.

"I always kept it with me, close to my heart," Ryan said as he held up the necklace, revealing the same ring hanging from it.

David reached out and touched the ring hanging from Ryan's neck, and in an instant, a rush of images flooded his mind. He saw Ryan grinning at him, and they were locked in a long, heartfelt hug. It was fleeting, but it left a mark.

"David? You alright?" Ryan asked, his concern etching lines on his face.

"Yeah, I think I just remembered something," David replied, his words cautious.

Ryan froze for a moment, and David worried he'd overwhelmed his friend. "A-Are you sure?"

"I reckon so. It was quick, but I saw you there, with your ring on, and we were hugging," David explained.

Ryan wrapped his arms around David, holding him tight. "Oh, David. I'm so chuffed. How are you feeling?"

"Like there was a rocket launch in my head. It's hurting a bit, Ry," David admitted. He wasn't sure why he'd started calling Ryan that, but it felt right, and Ryan didn't seem to mind.

"Do you need to lie down again?" Ryan asked, and David nodded. Ryan helped him back onto the couch. "Need anything else?"

"Just stay with me, please," David requested, and Ryan nodded, draping a blanket over him.

The last thing David felt before drifting off was Ryan's lips pressing a gentle kiss to his forehead.

11

David

D AVID WAS RUDELY AWAKENED by a series of relentless licks on his face. He blinked his eyes open to find Ryan holding Tyson in front of him, the cheeky cat going to town on his morning bath.

"You little rascal," David grumbled, turning away from the feline tongue assault. He heard Ryan chuckle, which made David crack a smile.

"How're you feeling now?" Ryan asked, concern lacing his voice.

David pondered for a moment, turning to see Ryan looking all worried while still holding Tyson like he was a baby. The sight was so daft that David couldn't help but burst into laughter. After a moment of confusion, Ryan joined in, and they were both laughing like a pair of loons.

"Yeah, I reckon I'm feeling better now," David finally managed to say through his giggles.

"Brilliant. Ready to head to the doctor's, then?" Ryan inquired.

David stretched and sat up. "What's the time?"

Ryan chuckled again. "Just a bit before lunch."

David nodded and got up. "Do we have time for a spot of lunch before that?"

"You're always hungry, aren't you?" Ryan teased, to which David simply nodded with a grin. "Well, we've got a bit of time. But we ought to get a move on."

Ryan helped David to his feet, making him feel like a right princess. They got ready in a flash, and David made sure to fill Tyson's water bowl before they left.

"So, where are you taking me for lunch?" David asked as they stood close enough for him to feel Ryan's body warmth, which made his throat go dry.

"I could take you to your favorite American diner, if you fancy?" Ryan suggested.

David's stomach rumbled at the thought. "Sounds good. Where's this place, then?"

Ryan flashed a charming smile. "It's over in Ealing Broadway. Let's get a move on."

With a gentle tug, Ryan took David's hand and led him over to where their Uber was waiting to whisk them away.

They arrived at Limeyard in Ealing Broadway, and David couldn't help but notice how unique it looked from the outside.

Stepping inside with Ryan, David was hit with some seriously chill American vibes. The place had this cool mix of rustic and industrial going on. The walls sported vintage wooden paneling, giving off a cozy, lived-in vibe. Edison bulbs hung from the ceiling, casting a warm, laid-back atmosphere. The floor was a throwback, part hardwood and part checkered tiles – pure retro charm.

Seating was a mishmash of different chairs and booths, each with its own character. Tables flaunted classic red-and-white checkered tablecloths, complete with those old-school condiment dispensers right in the middle.

Towards the back, an open kitchen showcased the magic – burgers sizzling, fries frying – making your stomach rumble in anticipation. And the walls were a trip down memory lane, covered in vintage posters, neon signs, and black-and-white photos of good ol' American nostalgia.

Yeah, Limeyard was like stepping into a time machine, with a side of good grub.

"Wow, this is something else. But in a good way," David remarked, finally recovering from his initial awe.

Ryan chuckled. "Yeah, it's a lot, but that's why you loved it."

They didn't have to wait long before a waitress appeared and led them to their seats, opting for a quieter spot in the back.

As they settled in, Ryan's phone pinged.

"That might be important," David pointed out once the waitress left them with their menus.

"Nah, I'll deal with it later," Ryan replied, his face betraying a hint of frustration. David noticed but decided not to pry, merely nodding in understanding.

After a moment, Ryan took a deep breath and locked eyes with David.

"You know, David," he began, his voice filled with emotion, "there's this memory at Limeyard that's always stuck with me."

David looked up from the menu. The soft, warm light from the Edison bulbs above made Ryan's face even more inviting, like he was about to share a secret.

"We were here on a cold winter night," Ryan continued, his gaze steady, "just like tonight. We snagged this very table, and you ordered your usual – that burger with extra pickles and those sweet potato fries you can't resist."

David's heart skipped a beat as he listened, feeling like he was peering through a fog, trying to grasp a memory that remained elusive.

Ryan kept going, a small smile on his face, "When the food came, your eyes lit up. I remember thinking how lucky I was to be right here with you. It was just a simple meal, but it felt like the whole world faded away, leaving just us."

Listening to Ryan's words, David felt the memory pressing against his mind, like a faint echo. He could almost smell the food, hear their laughter, and feel the touch of their hands brushing as they reached for fries.

Before he could fully embrace the memory, the waitress appeared, snapping them back to reality. She took their orders, and as she left, David turned back to Ryan, yearning in his eyes, eager to hear the rest of the story.

Ryan maintained eye contact. "And then," he said, his tone sincere, "you leaned in and told me it was one of the happiest moments of your life."

David's smile dimmed as he grappled with the weight of his amnesia. He wished he could remember, to share in those emotions and experiences that Ryan held dear. In that moment, the cozy ambiance of Limeyard seemed tinged with a sense of loss, a reminder of what remained locked away in his mind.

Their food arrived, and they dug in. Ryan had been spot on; the food was fantastic, and David found himself looking forward to future visits here.

After finishing their meal, David decided to ask for the bill, but then it hit him like a ton of bricks – he wasn't sure if he even had a wallet or a phone.

Ryan noticed the change in David's expression and asked, "What's wrong?"

David hesitated before asking, "Do you remember if I had a phone or a wallet by any chance?"

"You did, but we never really asked about that when you were brought to the hospital. Don't worry, I'll ask the Detective as soon as we get back to your place tonight," Ryan reassured him.

David nodded, a sense of gratitude washing over him. "Thanks, Ry. I appreciate it."

Ryan offered to pay for their meal, and David hesitated, concerned that Ryan was spending too much on him.

"Are you sure?"

"Yeah, you're worth every pound, mate," Ryan said with a wink, causing David to blush.

They settled the bill and headed back to the hospital. Upon arrival, Ryan turned to David and placed a reassuring hand on his shoulder.

"You're going to be okay, yeah?" Ryan said.

David appreciated the sentiment, even though he hadn't voiced his fears about the upcoming doctor's appointment.

"I know," he replied, grateful for Ryan's unwavering support.

As they walked into St. Thomas' Hospital in London, David couldn't help but notice that distinct hospital smell – you know, that antiseptic and disinfectant combo that always made him feel a bit queasy. It was the kind of scent that screamed doctors, needles, and a touch of anxiety.

The corridors were bustling with activity, nurses in their crisp white uniforms, doctors in lab coats, and patients of all sorts. The overhead lights beamed down with a fluorescent intensity that felt like it belonged to a different universe compared to the outside world.

David's heart began a drumroll of nerves, and he couldn't shake the feeling of being a fish out of water.

But with Ryan right there, his hand firmly on David's shoulder, it was like having a human security blanket. Ryan's presence, his cool and collected vibe, was like a stabilizer in the chaos of the hospital setting.

As they navigated the hospital's labyrinthine halls, David's emotions were on a wild rollercoaster ride. Fear of what the doctors might uncover during his examination battled with hope that maybe, just maybe, things were improving.

Despite the intimidating surroundings, Ryan's unwavering support and reassuring presence made David feel like he had an anchor in the storm. It was a reminder that he wasn't facing this journey of rediscovery on his own.

Eventually, they arrived at the reception area. Ryan stepped forward to chat with the nurse, and soon they were directed to Doctor Christiansen's office.

They gave a quick knock and entered to find the doctor engrossed in his computer work. He turned with a welcoming smile.

"Ah, there you guys are. Please, have a seat," the doctor said, and they took the offered chairs.

"Hey, Doctor, everything running smoothly around here?" Ryan kicked off the conversation.

"Everything is well. I should be asking both of you that. Tell me everything," the doctor replied.

David glanced at Ryan, who gave him an encouraging nod. "I've been getting these headaches, a couple of times a day, but they weren't unbearable," David started, recounting his recent experiences with dreams and glimpses of returning memories.

The doctor leaned back thoughtfully. "Memories have a funny way of making a comeback when you least expect them. We can view that as a positive sign of progress." He then turned to Ryan. "Whatever you're doing, it's working. As for the headaches, there might still be some lingering effects from your recent ordeal."

David nodded, absorbing the doctor's words. "So, is it time to bid farewell to the bandages today?" He asked hopefully.

"Absolutely, let's have a gander at it," the doctor replied.

David hadn't caught a glimpse of his hair or head for a good few days, so the curiosity was eating at him. What kind of scar or damage had he picked up? Doctor Christiansen carefully unwound the bandages, and David kept his eyes shut, bracing himself for whatever sight awaited him when he dared to look.

But then, Ryan's sudden gasp in front of him sent a ripple of nervousness through David. He couldn't help but ask, "Is it really that grim?"

Ryan offered a gentle smile and playfully ruffled his hair. "Nah, want to take a peek?"

David nodded, and Ryan whipped out his phone, flipping the camera around so David could see his own reflection. He couldn't help but notice a few bare patches around the stitches on his head. "Guess I'll be going for the full head shave, huh?"

"Don't sweat it. I'll give you a hand with that," Ryan said without missing a beat.

"You'd do that?" David felt touched by Ryan's offer.

"Of course. That's what mates are for."

"Yeah, mates," David grinned.

They wrapped up their visit to the doctor's office soon after.

"Here, chuck on my hoodie for the journey back," Ryan suggested, taking off his hoodie. David couldn't help but notice a bit of skin on Ryan's stomach as he peeled it off.

David promptly turned his gaze away to avoid making a total idiot of himself, but his cheeks still burned.

"Here you go," Ryan handed him the hoodie, revealing that he was only wearing a tank top underneath, which was, well, kind of distracting.

Bloody hell, the bloke's fit.

"T-Thanks," David stammered as he slipped on the hoodie, relishing the faint scent of Ryan lingering on the fabric.

"Right then, let's make our way home," Ryan said, pulling him into a one-armed hug.

12

Ryan

"SIT STILL," Ryan said firmly, his tone more Dad-like than a hairstylist's.

He was right in the middle of giving David a new look, and his 'client' seemed to be having a hard time keeping still. Ryan had a hunch he might be in trouble once David's memory fully returned. The guy was quite attached to his hair.

After the visit to the doctor's, Ryan's mood had improved considerably. Doctor Christiansen's diagnosis had injected a much-needed dose of hope into the situation. Progress, no matter how small, was still progress.

Ryan sympathized with David when he saw the scar and stitches on his head. He couldn't fully grasp the pain and confusion his best mate was going through, but he was determined to be the steady support David needed.

"How can I sit still when you're back there chuckling?" David protested. He clutched Tyson, who was squirming in his lap, like a lifeline.

Well, maybe Ryan was having a bit of a laugh, especially since David was acting like a jittery cat, treating Tyson as if the cat were a magical amulet.

"Don't blame me, mate. You look like the Dalmatian-loving version of a cat lady," Ryan teased, careful not to push his luck too far. Becoming a human scratching post wasn't on his agenda for the day.

"What's that supposed to mean?" David retorted, sounding mildly irritated.

Ryan decided it was wiser to halt the teasing before Tyson's claws got involved. "Alright, alright, I'll be on my best behaviour as long as you stay put," he conceded.

The haircut didn't take long to finish. Ryan was content with the results, but he was more concerned about David's reaction.

"What do you think?" Ryan asked, his anxiety creeping up.

David studied his reflection in the mirror for what felt like an eternity. Ryan held his breath, silently praying he hadn't messed up.

"I love it. Did I usually have long hair before all this?" David inquired, a genuine smile breaking across his face.

Ryan let out a relieved sigh. "Yeah, you never let it get this short. But I'm glad you like it."

David turned towards him, that radiant grin still firmly in place. "Thank you! Maybe when I get my memories back, I'll be open to keeping it short for a while."

David did look rather dashing with the new haircut, and Ryan couldn't help but have this weird urge to reach out and pat his head. It was a bit strange, and Ryan had to give himself a mental shake to get rid of those unexpected thoughts. He couldn't afford to be fantasizing about David like that.

Ryan hadn't dared to read any more of the letter David had written for him. It was a lot to take in. Now that he knew how David truly felt about him, he was sort of at a loss about how to handle it.

"Come on, let's tidy up here, and then we can catch a movie before I head out," Ryan suggested.

David seemed a bit disappointed. "You're leaving?"

"Yeah, I've got a meeting with the Detective who's handling your case. Need to get some updates and maybe ask about your phone and wallet. Want to tag along?" Ryan offered.

David shook his head. "Nah, I think I've had enough excitement for the past couple of days, and I'm not sure I'm ready to hear what he has to say."

Ryan was genuinely proud of David for putting his own well-being first.

After giving David a fresh look with the haircut, they settled comfortably on the living room couch. The room was dimly lit, the soft glow of the TV casting a warm light on their faces. They decided to watch a horror movie, and David picked one out. Ryan grinned and nodded, even though he knew David couldn't recall his love for horror.

As the movie began, Ryan couldn't help but feel a sense of nostalgia. He turned to David and said, "You know, horror used to be your thing, mate. You were really into it. Loved the thrill, the suspense, and watching me jump out of my skin."

David looked at Ryan with a curious expression. "Really? I used to be into horror?"

Ryan chuckled, reminiscing about their shared experiences. "Absolutely. You were the one who'd drag me into watching those classic scary flicks. You'd have a proper laugh when I'd flinch."

David furrowed his brow, clearly intrigued. "I did that?"

Ryan nodded, his smile filled with fond memories. "Regularly, mate. We'd order some takeaway, set up a little horror movie marathon, and you'd be in stitches watching me jump."

David's eyes started to sparkle with a mix of curiosity and nostalgia. "We did that?"

Ryan nodded, feeling the warmth of their shared memories fill the room. "Yeah, mate. Good times, isn't it? But, well, you know... with everything that's happened…"

With David's head resting on his shoulder while they watched the horror movie, Ryan couldn't help but feel a swirl of emotions. It was a simple, everyday gesture, but it held a deeper meaning for him.

Ryan sensed a closeness and camaraderie between them, as if they were just two pals hanging out, despite their past being clouded by amnesia. David's presence beside him was comforting, and the weight of his head on Ryan's shoulder was strangely reassuring.

As the movie played on, Ryan subtly adjusted his position to make sure David was comfy. There wasn't much need for words; their shared silence spoke volumes. In that ordinary moment, Ryan hoped that maybe, just maybe, some of the lost memories would find their way back to David, and they could make new ones together.

Ryan observed David's slow and steady breathing, a sure sign that David had dozed off. It warmed his heart to see his friend sleeping so peacefully.

Gently, he tucked a blanket around David before getting ready to head out. Ryan casually slipped on a pair of shoes, grabbed his jacket, and made his way to meet Detective Wayne at the local coffee shop for their regular check-in on David's case.

Although he wasn't officially part of the investigation, Ryan had taken it upon himself to stay involved. His loyalty to David was rock-solid, and he was ready to go to great lengths to help his friend recover his lost memories

Ryan sat in the cozy little coffee shop, sipping on his cappuccino, awaiting Detective Wayne.

He didn't have to wait long as Detective Wayne walked in a couple of minutes later, and Ryan greeted him with a nod. "Detective, thanks for meeting me."

The detective pulled out a chair, his expression serious. "No problem, Ryan. How's David holding up?"

Ryan leaned back in his chair, letting out a sigh. "It's been a real rollercoaster, Detective. He's struggling, and it's completely understandable. The amnesia has hit him hard, and it's tough to watch."

Detective Wayne nodded in sympathy. "I can imagine. Any signs of his memory coming back?"

Ryan shook his head. "Not much, Detective. There have been some glimpses, but it's a frustrating process for him. I'm doing my best to support him, but it's a tough road."

The detective reached into his briefcase and took out a folder, placing it on the table. "Well, we've got some updates on the case. It's been a challenging one, and progress has been slow. But we've managed to create a composite sketch of a potential suspect based on a recent eyewitness account."

Ryan leaned forward, examining the sketch with interest. It was a rough likeness, but it was a tangible lead, something they hadn't had before. "This is a start, at least. Do you think it matches the attacker?"

Detective Wayne shrugged. "Hard to say, Ryan. Eyewitness accounts can be hit or miss, and the sketch is pretty generic. But it's a lead, and we're following up on it."

Ryan understood the complexities of the investigation and nodded. "What's our next move, Detective?"

"We'll share the sketch with local law enforcement and maybe release it to the media," Detective Wayne explained. "We're hoping it might jog someone's memory or prompt them to come forward with information."

Ryan agreed with the plan, knowing that even a small lead could make a difference. "Let's hope for the best. David deserves to know who did this to him."

Detective Wayne's expression softened as he nodded. "I couldn't agree more, Ryan. We won't stop until we find answers."

"Detective, I wanted to ask about David's phone and wallet," Ryan began. "Are they still in police custody?"

Detective Wayne confirmed, "Yes, they're currently locked up in our evidence locker. We can't release them until we've thoroughly examined everything."

Ryan had expected as much. "Is there any way we can speed up the process? David's eager to know if there's anything on his phone that might help with the case."

Detective Wayne sighed, "I understand your urgency, Ryan. I'll do my best to expedite things, but we have to follow proper procedure to preserve the evidence."

Ryan appreciated Detective Wayne's willingness to assist and nodded. "Thank you, Detective. I'll update David on the situation. It might give him some peace of mind to know we're making progress."

They continued discussing the case, and Ryan couldn't help but feel a renewed determination. He knew the road ahead would be tough, but he was committed to being there for David every step of the way.

Ryan glanced at his phone and saw it was nearly dinner time. Realizing there wasn't enough time to cook, he made a quick U-turn and headed to the nearest Tesco. He grabbed some sandwiches, knowing it wasn't a fancy meal, but it was all he could afford at the moment. He'd have to dip into his savings for a while, but it was worth it for David.

As he was about to check out, he spotted David's favorite sweets. He couldn't resist, knowing how happy they made David. A smile crept onto his face as he remembered those moments.

He added the sweets to his basket and paid for everything, which came to about twenty quid. With the groceries in a plastic bag, he headed back home.

Standing at David's front door, groceries in hand, he felt a pang of worry as he heard faint whimpering from inside. Fumbling for his keys, he hurriedly unlocked the door. David had been asleep when he left, and the thought of his friend in distress made him anxious.

Entering the flat, the whimpering grew louder, guiding him to the source. Following the sound, he found David huddled on the couch. Relief washed over him; David was safe, even though he was far from okay. David's face was pale, his eyes squeezed shut, and he held a pillow tightly to his chest as if seeking comfort.

"David," Ryan called gently, setting the groceries on the table. He sat down next to his friend. "Hey, it's me, Ryan. You're safe now."

David's eyes fluttered open, a glimmer of fear fading as recognition set in. He blinked as if trying to clear a lingering nightmare.

"Ryan?" David's voice was weak, and he looked disoriented.

"Yeah, it's me," Ryan reassured him, placing a hand on David's shoulder. "You had another nightmare, mate. You're okay now."

David shivered, despite the room's warmth. "I… I don't remember…"

Ryan offered a sympathetic smile. "It's alright. Bad dreams can be like that sometimes. Do you want to talk about it?"

David hesitated, then glanced at the grocery bag on the table. "What's all this?"

Ryan decided to lighten the mood for a moment. "I got us some sandwiches for dinner. And your favourite sweets." He held up the bag of treats with a playful grin.

A hint of a smile appeared on David's lips. "You remembered?"

"Of course, I did," Ryan said, relieved to see David's mood improve, if only a bit.

They ate their sandwiches in silence, the comforting sound of chewing filling the room. David seemed to relax with every bite, finding solace in the familiar taste.

After they finished, Ryan cleared their plates and turned his attention back to David. "Now, about that dream. If you want to share, I'm here to listen."

David hesitated for a moment before sighing. "It was… confusing. I don't even know if it was a memory or just my mind playing tricks on me."

Ryan nodded, encouraging him to continue.

"I was… shaking, and someone was talking to me and called me a slur," David began, his voice soft and uncertain.

Ryan's heart sank. He knew David's journey to regain his memories would be filled with confusing and distressing moments, but it didn't make it any easier to witness his friend's struggle.

"I'm sorry you had to go through that," Ryan said sincerely. "But remember, it's just a dream. We'll figure all this out together."

David met Ryan's gaze, gratitude evident in his eyes. "Thanks, Ryan. You've been so patient with me, even when I can't remember anything properly."

Ryan smiled, his concern for David matched by his determination to support his friend. "We're in this together, David. You don't have to go through it alone."

David nodded, and they sat in the quiet living room, finding comfort in each other's presence.

13

David

DAVID SLOWLY BLINKED HIS EYES OPEN, feeling more refreshed than he had in a while. It took him a moment to remember where he was, but the cozy familiarity of his own room quickly reassured him.

As he shifted in bed, David noticed something unusual. He wasn't alone. Turning his head, he saw Ryan sleeping soundly on the floor beside him, a makeshift bed of blankets and pillows.

David couldn't help but wonder how he had ended up in bed. He certainly didn't remember being carried. The idea of Ryan carrying him and tucking him in was comforting in some way.

Deciding to wake Ryan up, David gently nudged his friend's shoulder. "Ryan, wake up," he whispered.

Ryan stirred, blinking his eyes open and squinting against the morning light. He looked slightly disoriented for a moment before recognition set in.

"Morning," David said, a soft smile playing on his lips. "Why are you sleeping on the floor? There's enough space on the bed."

Ryan yawned and stretched, rubbing the sleep from his eyes. "Oh, I didn't want to disturb you. Thought you might need a good night's sleep after the nightmares."

"You didn't have to do that, you know."

Ryan chuckled and sat up, leaning against the edge of the bed. "Your comfort is my priority. Besides, the floor wasn't all that bad."

David shook his head in disbelief. "You're too good for me, Ryan."

With a smile, Ryan glanced at his phone, which was resting on the bedside table. It suddenly started ringing. He hesitated for a moment but eventually answered the call.

"Hello?" Ryan said, his voice cautious.

David listened to Ryan's side of the conversation, trying to piece together what was happening. He couldn't hear the other person, but he sensed that Ryan's expression was growing more serious by the second.

After a few minutes, Ryan hung up and turned to David with a sigh. "That was my boss. They need me to come in to the office today for something urgent."

David frowned, concerned about the interruption to their routine. "Is everything okay? Do you have to go?"

Ryan ran a hand through his hair, clearly conflicted. "Yeah, it's work-related, and I don't think I can postpone it. But I don't want to leave you alone for too long."

"It's fine, Ryan. I'll be okay. You've done so much for me already."

Ryan's eyes conveyed his gratitude as he stood up and stretched again. "I promise I won't be gone for long."

As Ryan got ready to leave, David couldn't help but reflect on the complex feelings swirling inside him. He was starting to care deeply for Ryan.

With a sigh, David pushed those thoughts aside and offered Ryan a reassuring smile. "Go on, handle your work stuff. I'll keep myself busy here."

Ryan nodded appreciatively, grabbed his coat, and headed for the door. Before leaving, he turned back to David. "Take care, mate. I'll be back as soon as I can."

David watched Ryan exit the flat, feeling a sense of emptiness settle in. He couldn't deny that Ryan's presence had become a comforting constant in his life, a lifeline as he navigated the maze of his lost memories.

As he wandered around the flat, David couldn't help but think about his feelings for Ryan. It was a tricky situation, especially since he believed Ryan was straight. The last thing he wanted was to jeopardise their friendship or make things awkward between them.

David decided to keep his emotions in check and focus on the day ahead. He occupied himself with small tasks around the flat, tidying up and organizing things. Despite the uncertainty of his past, he was determined to create a sense of order and control in his present.

David sat on the couch, casually flipping through the pages of a book he'd found on the shelf. The soft, warm glow of the room gave it a peaceful ambiance, a welcome distraction from the constant puzzle of his lost memories.

As he idly turned another page, a small photograph slipped from between the book's pages, landing in his lap with an almost casual grace. David raised an eyebrow, curiosity piqued. It was a picture of him and Ryan, their genuine smiles frozen in a moment of pure happiness. They stood before a beautiful landscape, bathed in the golden hues of a setting sun.

The sight of the photograph triggered something in David, a memory trying to claw its way out. His head throbbed suddenly, sharp pain shooting through his temples. Wincing, he brought a hand to his forehead, trying to make sense of the chaotic images and emotions flooding his mind.

Laughter echoed around them, mingling with the gentle rustling of leaves in the breeze. David felt a sense of contentment that he couldn't quite explain, as if this moment held a special place in his heart.

He could hear Ryan's voice, rich with warmth and friendship. "David, you've got to see this view. It's incredible." David turned to see Ryan standing there, a wide grin on his face, the sun turning his hair into a halo of gold.

The two of them stood side by side, taking in the breathtaking scenery. The world felt perfect in that moment, and David couldn't imagine being anywhere else.

Ryan turned to him, that familiar mischievous glint in his eyes. "Race you back to the cabin?" David laughed, the competition between them as natural as breathing.

As they raced back, the world blurred around them, and David couldn't help but think that this was what true friendship felt like—pure, unadulterated joy.

But the memories were elusive, slipping away like sand through his fingers. David closed his eyes and took a deep breath, trying to regain his composure. The pain in his head gradually eased, leaving behind a frustrating sense of longing.

The photograph in his hand held a promise—a promise of a deeper connection, a bond that went beyond the confines of his amnesia. It was a bond of shared moments, of laughter and friendship. David knew he couldn't give up on his quest to uncover the truth about his past.

With a resigned sigh, he carefully tucked the photograph back between the book's pages and closed it. Ryan had been his rock, his unwavering support, and together, they would unravel the mysteries of his forgotten past, one memory at a time. But the pain in his head served as a harsh reminder that the road ahead wouldn't be easy.

14

David

DAVID WAS IN THE MIDDLE OF MAKING TEA when the doorbell rang. He glanced at the clock and realized it had only been a few hours since Ryan had left.

He couldn't have returned so quickly, could he?

Setting aside his tea-making, David walked hesitantly to the front door, his curiosity mingled with uncertainty. The doorbell rang again, urging him to make a decision. With a deep breath, he opened the door.

Before him stood a man slightly taller than himself, dressed in a suit that spoke of formality.

"David?" the man inquired.

"Yes? Can I help you?" David replied, his expression a mix of confusion and wariness.

"Are you having a laugh, mate? You gonna let me in?" the man asked with a hint of impatience.

David's skepticism lingered, but he decided to allow the man inside. Leading him to the kitchen, David took a seat and gestured for the visitor to do the same.

"Sorry, I don't really remember who you are. So if you could please tell me what we are to each other, I would be grateful," David stated bluntly.

The man appeared bewildered. "I'm sorry?"

"I… I don't know what you've heard, but I lost my memory after an attack one night," David explained, his voice tinged with frustration as he recalled the painful ordeal.

"Attack? David. Tell me what's going on. Why was I not told about this? Is this why you weren't answering your phone the last couple of days, and the hair?" the man fired off questions in rapid succession.

"One question at a time, please. My head can only handle so much these days. Why don't you start with your name?" David suggested, prompting the man to comply.

"I am Nicholas Laurent. Nic for short. Or what you used to call me, Nicky. I am your manager and one of your closest friends," Nicky revealed.

"Ryan told me that I was a stylist. Does that mean that I work for you?" David inquired.

"Yes, you do, and you're one of the best stylists I have. I wonder why Ryan hadn't told me about this," Nicky mused.

"He said he was going to call you, but I suppose he's been busy here trying to help me," David replied softly.

"Ryan's been here?" Nicky asked, genuine surprise coloring his features.

"He's been staying here. He just left because work called him in," David confirmed.

Nicky nodded, processing the new information. "Do you remember what happened?"

David sighed, a hint of frustration evident in his voice. "No, I don't remember anything. The doctor said that I have Dissociative Amnesia due to the severity of the trauma I suffered. But Ryan and my parents told me the gist of it." David recounted the details as best he could.

Nicky's eyes welled up with tears as David finished his narrative. He moved closer, embracing David, who reciprocated the hug, grateful for the support.

"I am so sorry, David. I should have been here," Nicky whispered.

David pulled away gently, a reassuring smile on his face. "Nothing to be sorry about. It wasn't your fault."

"Well, if you need my help with anything, just let me know," Nicky offered.

"Actually, there is one thing," David began, capturing Nicky's attention.

"What is it?" Nicky asked, curiosity piqued.

"I want to do something nice for Ryan. And I was thinking about cooking," David revealed, his eyes reflecting determination and a hint of excitement.

"Are you sure you want to do this, David?" Nicky asked, his voice laced with concern. "You've been through quite a lot recently, and cooking might be a bit much at the moment."

David shook his head. "No, Nicky, I need to do something for Ryan. He's been incredible, and I want to show him my gratitude. Besides, I used to enjoy cooking, didn't I?"

Nicky's warm smile appeared, a flicker of fondness in his eyes. "You certainly did, David. You used to whip up the most delicious dishes for the team. Cooking was your way of bringing people together."

"I want to do that for Ryan."

"Alright, then. Let's see what we can come up with. You kept your recipes somewhere in this kitchen, didn't you?"

Feeling inspired, David joined Nicky in searching the kitchen. Cupboards were opened, drawers were examined, and shelves were scoured. It didn't take long before David's eyes fell upon a worn, recipe-filled book tucked away in a corner.

His heart swelled with a mix of nostalgia and gratitude as he picked up the book. "Is this it?"

Nicky's eyes gleamed with satisfaction. "That's the one, David! Now, let's see what culinary masterpiece you can create for Ryan."

David flipped through the pages, pausing at one recipe that had a star scribbled next to it. "How about this one? It must have been special if I marked it."

Nicky leaned in to take a look at the chosen recipe and grinned. "Pasta with homemade tomato sauce and basil? That sounds delicious. Let's do it."

Excitement welled up within David as he read through the ingredients and instructions. The thought of preparing a homemade meal for Ryan filled him with anticipation.

"Great choice, David," Nicky said, offering an encouraging smile. "Now, let's make a shopping list and head to the grocery store."

David nodded eagerly, and they began jotting down the necessary ingredients. It was a comforting feeling, going through the motions of preparing a meal, even if he couldn't remember the details. It was like catching a fleeting glimpse into the life he used to have.

Once the list was complete, they ventured to the nearby grocery store. The scent of fresh produce and baked goods greeted them as they entered, and David couldn't help but feel a sense of nostalgia wash over him.

As they made their way through the aisles, Nicky guiding him through the store, David's head began to throb with an intense pain. He winced, clutching his temple as he leaned against a shelf for support.

"David, are you alright?" Nicky asked, his voice filled with concern.

David's vision blurred for a moment, and he struggled to form a coherent response. "I... I don't know, Nicky. My head... it hurts."

Nicky steadied him, his arm around David's shoulder as he helped him find a nearby bench to sit on. "Take deep breaths, David. We'll get through this."

David squeezed his eyes shut, attempting to control the pain that radiated through his head. He couldn't remember anything, just a massive migraine that seemed to pierce through his very thoughts.

After a few minutes, the pain began to subside, leaving David feeling drained and disoriented. He opened his eyes to see Nicky's worried expression.

"Are you feeling any better?" Nicky asked gently.

David nodded weakly, his voice a mere whisper. "Yeah, it's passing. I'm sorry, Nicky, I didn't mean to cause a scene."

With the throbbing pain in his head subsiding, David and Nicky decided to return home, their grocery trip cut short. Nicky paid for the ingredients, and they headed back to the flat.

Once the migraine had subsided, David felt a renewed determination to prepare a special meal for Ryan. He looked at Nicky, who had been there for him throughout the day, with a sense of gratitude.

"Nicky, would you mind helping me set up the kitchen before Ryan gets home?"

Nicky nodded with a warm smile. "Of course, David. I'd be happy to help. What can I do?"

David began to outline his plan. "Well, first, let's make sure all the necessary ingredients are laid out. Then, we'll get the cooking utensils ready, and I'll need your assistance with some of the tasks. But don't worry, I promise to yell for help if I need it."

Nicky chuckled. "Let's make this meal for Ryan something special."

They both set to work, gathering the ingredients on the kitchen counter. David carefully checked the recipe in his old cookbook, making sure they hadn't missed anything.

As they got down to cooking, David couldn't help but feel a mix of excitement and nerves. Cooking used to be a real joy for him, you know, like his happy place. But now, with his memory gone, it's like starting from scratch, and that's a bit scary.

Nicky, always the supportive mate, said, "Come on, David. Cooking's just like riding a bike."

David managed a little grin, grateful for Nicky's pep talk. "I hope so, Nicky. I just want this meal to be a real treat for Ryan."

With all the ingredients laid out, they got to work chopping veggies, herbs, and getting the sauce bubbling away on the stove. David moved carefully, following the cookbook's written instructions like it was his lifeline.

Nicky was a real gem, giving him tips and lending a hand when needed. He had a knack for making things seem less daunting.

As they worked together, David's mind wandered to these hazy memories he couldn't quite grab onto. It was like he could almost taste the dishes he'd made before and hear the laughter of pals and colleagues in the kitchen. Those memories were like little teases, just out of his reach.

The smell of the tomato sauce simmering away filled the kitchen, and David felt a proper sense of achievement. He was doing this all for Ryan, his mate who'd stuck with him through thick and thin.

Checking the clock, David said, "Ryan should be back any minute now. We're making good progress, Nicky. Thanks a bunch for helping me out with this."

Nicky beamed, wiping his hands on a tea towel. "No worries, David. It's been a blast."

15

Ryan

AS RYAN LEFT DAVID'S FLAT, he couldn't stop thinking about the row he'd had with his boss earlier. Craig had been proper short on the phone, telling Ryan that Elle was causing a scene in the office and he had to sort it out. Ryan knew it was a right pain, but he couldn't let Elle mess up his job.

On his way back to Hackney, Ryan's frustration kept building up. He liked Elle, no doubt about it, but her constant doubts and accusations were driving him mad. He needed some breathing space away from all this relationship drama.

When he got to the gym, he swiped his ID card to get in. Andy, the front desk guy, looked well fed up already.

"Ryan, you won't believe what's happening," Andy sighed, walking over. "Elle's in Craig's office, and she's… well, you know how she can be."

Ryan nodded, not thrilled about the situation. "Yeah, I've got a pretty good idea. Cheers, Andy."

He made his way to Craig's office, taking a deep breath to brace himself. He had to stay cool and collected; Elle's jealousy wasn't going to get the best of him. He knocked on the door, and Craig called him in.

As Ryan walked in, he felt the tension in the room. Elle was pacing, her face all flushed with anger. Craig looked like he'd had enough.

"Ryan, thank goodness you're here," Craig muttered, running a hand through his hair. "Elle won't listen to reason. Maybe you can talk some sense into her."

Elle turned to Ryan, eyes blazing with fury. "So, you finally decided to show up."

Ryan clenched his fists, trying to stay calm. "Elle, we need to talk, but not here. Let's go to my place. We can sort this out in private."

Elle scoffed, dripping with sarcasm. "Oh, how convenient for you, Ryan. I bet you'd love that, wouldn't you?"

Ryan's patience was wearing thin, but he kept his tone steady. "This ain't about what I want, Elle. It's about fixing our problems. I can't keep doing this, and I don't want our relationship falling apart because of unfounded accusations."

Elle hesitated for a sec before reluctantly agreeing with a begrudging nod. "Fine, let's go to your place. But don't think this changes anything, Ryan."

They left Craig's office, Ryan keenly aware of the curious looks from his colleagues. He couldn't help feeling embarrassed and frustrated by Elle's drama at his workplace.

When they got outside, Ryan hailed a cab, and they sat there in silence, the tension thick as a brick. Neither of them wanted to break that awkward quiet.

They finally arrived at Ryan's flat in Hackney. Ryan held the door open for Elle, and she walked in all defiant-like. Ryan followed her and closed the door.

In the living room, they stood there, the air so heavy with unsaid stuff.

Elle's eyes bore into Ryan's, a mix of hurt and anger. "Ryan, we need to talk about what's been happening. I can't keep pretending everything's fine."

Ryan sighed, looking well knackered. "I know, Elle. It's just... these last few days have been a right mess, and I didn't want to argue in public."

Elle crossed her arms. "That's not an excuse, Ryan. You've been avoiding me, ignoring my calls and texts. I need to know the truth."

Ryan's jaw tightened, meeting her accusing gaze. "Elle, it's just a mate who needed my support. There's nothing more to it."

But Elle wasn't buying it. "There's something going on, and I won't stand for it."

Ryan's patience was running out, and he could feel his temper rising. He knew he had to tread carefully because he couldn't spill the beans about David, not now, not like this. "Elle, please, you're overthinking this."

Elle took a step closer, her eyes filling with tears. "Then prove it, Ryan. Prove you're not hiding anything from me."

Ryan hesitated, torn between protecting David and saving his relationship with Elle. He knew that telling the truth could risk everything, but Elle's stare left him no choice.

"Elle, I can't do that," Ryan said firmly. "This ain't about keeping secrets; it's about trust. If you can't trust me, maybe we need to think about our relationship."

The words hung in the air, heavy with their unresolved problems. Elle's face twisted with anger and desperation. "Are you really giving me an ultimatum, Ryan?"

Ryan's voice was steady as he replied, "I'm not giving you an ultimatum, Elle. I'm asking you to trust me, just like I trust you. Without trust, we've got nothing to build on."

Elle's eyes filled with tears as she took a step back, her anger giving way to vulnerability. "I just need to know, Ryan. I need to know if you're being honest with me."

Ryan sighed, feeling the weight of what he had to do. He couldn't risk losing Elle, but he also couldn't spill the beans about David. "Elle, I promise you, there's nothing shady with this mate. Please try to get it."

Tears streamed down Elle's face as she turned away, her voice shaky. "I can't, Ryan. I can't be in a relationship without trust. I need some time to think."

Ryan watched as Elle walked toward the door, a sense of helplessness washing over him. He didn't want to lose her, but he also couldn't betray David's trust. The room felt empty as she left, and he knew their relationship was hanging by a thread.

After that intense chat with Elle, Ryan needed a breather and a way to let off some steam. He decided to hit the gym. Grabbing his gym bag, he swapped his regular clothes for workout gear, and off he went. The gym was like his refuge — a place to escape the relationship drama he'd just waded through.

Stepping into the gym was like being enveloped in a familiar embrace. The mingling scents of sweat and determination hit him in the face, and honestly, it felt like coming home. He needed to shift his focus away from his rocky relationship, and a solid workout was the best remedy.

Craig, his boss, clocked his return and gave him a concerned look. "Ryan, you doing alright there?"

Ryan gave a weary nod, appreciating the concern. "Yeah, it was a bit of a rough one, Craig. But I'm here to sweat it out and get back on track."

Craig slapped him on the shoulder in a supportive, buddy-like manner. "That's the spirit, mate. Remember, we've got your back if you ever need anything."

With a grateful nod, Ryan headed over to the weights section. He needed to let off some steam, and the rhythmic clinking of weights was his therapy. Each repetition, each lift, helped him focus on the physical strain rather than the emotional chaos.

Time flew as he pushed himself to the limit, the sweat pouring and the effort demanding his complete attention. It was a much-needed escape from the tangled mess of his personal life.

After an intense workout, Ryan hit the showers. The warm water felt like a soothing embrace, washing away both the physical exhaustion and the emotional turmoil. He took his time, enjoying the peace and quiet of the locker room.

Feeling refreshed and ready for the world, Ryan knew he couldn't leave David hanging any longer. He'd promised they'd spend the evening together, and he intended to keep that commitment. Elle could wait; for now, he was eager to enjoy their dinner plans and put his relationship drama on the back burner.

16

Ryan

THE DELICIOUS SMELL OF HOME-COOKED FOOD greeted him as he walked in. It was like stepping into a cozy haven, a world away from the gym's sterile vibe.

David was all settled on the sofa, totally engrossed in an episode of the Great British Bake Off. Seeing David so chill and into his telly show made Ryan smile.

He couldn't resist teasing him, though. "Watching Bake Off, eh?"

David turned with a warm smile, looking genuinely happy. "Oh, busted. How was your day at work?"

Ryan paused for a sec, deciding to keep the whole Elle showdown to himself. No need to unload all that relationship drama on David right now.

"It was alright, you know, the usual grind. Got to sweat out some stress, which was what I needed."

David, always understanding, just nodded, not digging for more. "Well, I've been busy here too. My mate Nicky, the manager, popped round earlier, and we did some grocery shopping for dinner. Thought I'd surprise you."

Ryan's curiosity got the better of him. "Nicky came over?"

"Yeah, he didn't know what was going on, so he thought I was just blanking him."

Ryan felt a bit guilty. "What did you tell him?"

"I gave him the gist of it. Figured I owed him that much after everything."

Ryan's guilt deepened. "I'm sorry, I totally forgot to tell him."

David waved it off with a smile. "No worries. I knew you've been busy looking after me. No hard feelings."

I really don't deserve him.

Changing the topic, Ryan couldn't resist poking fun at David's cooking adventure. "So, you're the chef tonight? How'd you manage that?"

David's eyes lit up with excitement. "Well, I wanted to do something nice for you, and Nicky told me I've got a recipe book I made, so we used that."

Ryan couldn't help but laugh. "Sounds brilliant, David. Can't wait to see what you've whipped up. And Nicky's a good mate for lending a hand."

David beamed at the compliment, and Ryan couldn't help but feel dead lucky. "He is, and I'm well chuffed to have mates like you and Nicky around."

As they kept nattering and enjoying each other's company, Ryan couldn't help but be thankful for the stability and comfort David brought into his life. Even with all the Elle drama, being with David made him feel all calm and part of something.

They scoffed down the meal David had rustled up, and for a bit, it felt like all the stress from the outside world just melted away.

After they cleared the dinner table together, Ryan had this feeling that things were gonna be alright, at least for now.

They settled on the comfy living room sofa after their satisfying dinner, and David casually rested his head on Ryan's shoulder. It was a simple thing, but it had this feeling of ease and comfort, something they hadn't really had in their friendship before. Ryan couldn't help but like this newfound closeness and the change in how they were getting along.

Ryan's mind started wandering as he thought about this shift in their relationship. They'd never really been this close, not physically or emotionally. Now, after reading David's heartfelt letter, Ryan had a better idea why David had kept his distance before.

He couldn't help but wonder what all this meant. It was a bit of a head-scratcher, but at the same time, it made him feel all warm and content.

With everything they'd been through lately, Ryan thought it was time to bring up something he'd been thinking about. He asked David in a relaxed way, "So, what's the plan for tomorrow, David?"

David shifted a bit, sounding all calm and thoughtful. "I was thinking… I fancy going back to the place where that attack happened."

Ryan's eyebrows shot up, caught off guard by David wanting to revisit that tough and painful part of his past. He turned to David with a concerned look. "You sure about that, mate? It could be a real slog."

David met Ryan's gaze with a determined look. "Yeah, I know it won't be a walk in the park, but I need to face it, Ryan. I need to tackle my past."

Ryan was torn, wanting to shield David from the emotional turmoil this might bring but also respecting his mate's wishes. In the end, he couldn't refuse. "Alright, David. If that's what you want, we'll go together. I've got your back through thick and thin."

David's eyes sparkled with gratitude, and he gave a warm smile. "Cheers, Ryan. That means the world."

It didn't take long for David to nod off to dreamland. Ryan watched his friend, feeling a mix of affection, protectiveness, and some deep thinking.

It was a moment of quiet closeness, one that felt strangely right and comforting. Ryan couldn't deny the complexity of his feelings for David anymore. His initial confusion had evolved into a deeper understanding of his emotions, and he was slowly coming to terms with the idea that maybe his feelings for David weren't just platonic.

As he looked at David sleeping like a baby, Ryan thought about the uncertainties of what lay ahead.

Maybe he wasn't as straight as he once believed, but that was alright. What really mattered was the real connection he had with David and how they had each other's backs, no matter what.

In that peaceful moment, Ryan couldn't help but feel a sense of contentment and acceptance. No matter what the future had in store, he knew he was ready to face it with David by his side.

Ryan carefully picked David up and took him to his bedroom. He tucked him in and planted a gentle kiss on his forehead before turning off the lights and going back to the living room.

He noticed that box again, that pile of letters from David. He sighed, giving in to his curiosity. He picked one of the letters, one that looked like it had seen better days, and opened it up slowly.

Hey Ryan,

I hope you're doing good, mate. I can't believe we're both sixteen now. Time's flying by, isn't it? Anyway, there's something I've been wanting to talk to you about, and I figured now's as good a time as any.

You know, ever since we became friends, things have been... well, different. You've been like this constant ray of sunshine in my life. Your laugh, your smile - they've become my favourite things in the world. I look forward to the moments we share, the inside jokes, the late-night chats - it's like my day isn't complete without them.

But here's the thing, Ryan. Lately, I've realised that what I feel for you goes beyond just friendship. It's more profound, more intense, and I don't quite know how to put it into words. The truth is, I love you, mate. And I mean that in a way that's deeper than anything I've ever felt before.

I know this might be coming out of left field, and I don't want to drop a bombshell on you. It's just that these feelings have been growing inside me, silently, for a while now. I've tried to make sense of them, and the more I've thought about it, the clearer it's become.

Now, I'm not expecting you to feel the same way, and I don't want you to feel pressured or uncomfortable.

No matter how you feel about this, please know that I'm here for you. I'm not going anywhere. Whether we remain the closest of friends or if our paths take a different turn, you'll always have a special place in my heart.

I want to continue sharing the laughs, the adventures, and the ups and downs of life with you, Ryan. You're an incredible person, and nothing can change that.

So, mate, let's navigate this new chapter in our lives together, with honesty and openness. We've got an exciting journey ahead of us as we explore who we are and what the world has in store for us. And, who knows, maybe life has a few surprises in store for us as well.

Take care, Ryan, and remember, I'm just a chat or a call away whenever you're ready to talk.

No Matter what.

Catch you later,

David

P.S. I couldn't fit all this into one letter, but there's so much more I want to say.

"Oh, David, you lovely fool," Ryan murmured to himself, his voice all filled with a mix of feelings. He gently placed the letter back on the coffee table, his hands shaking a bit. Tyson, always in tune with his owner's emotions, jumped onto the couch and settled on Ryan's lap, offering up some nice, comforting purrs.

Ryan blinked back tears, not even realizing he'd been crying until a few drops landed on the letter, smudging the ink just a tad. He wiped his cheeks with the back of his hand, feeling this whirlwind of feelings stirring inside him.

Gently, Ryan picked up the letter again, handling it like something precious. He folded it back to where it belonged, taking a moment to soak in the words they'd shared.

I'm scared and excited that I'm starting to love you the same way, too.

With Tyson all cozy on his lap and David's words etched into his mind, Ryan couldn't ignore the big impact David had on his life. Love, he realized, was a beautiful and tangled thing, but he was ready to embrace it, whatever lay ahead.

17

David

"WE CAN ALWAYS HEAD BACK, YOU KNOW?" Ryan's words hung in the air.

David and Ryan found themselves at a Starbucks in Bond Street, sipping on coffee and munching on their breakfast. The smell of freshly brewed coffee and the city's lively bustle outside the café's windows created a cosy atmosphere.

David shifted in his seat, his gaze wandering to the vibrant streets of Central London.

Maybe Ryan's got a point, perhaps going back home would be the safer bet.

He couldn't fault his mate's concern, even if he teased him about it from time to time.

With a playful roll of his eyes, David replied, "Ryan, you're like a big brother on protection duty. I appreciate it, but I can't keep dodging my past. It's time to tackle it head-on."

"Yeah, I get it," Ryan admitted softly.

David valued Ryan's unwavering support. It had been the backbone of their friendship, and it meant the world to him.

"Absolutely. We're in this together," David said.

During their chat, David couldn't help but notice a change in Ryan's attitude. There was this extra layer of tenderness and affection, both in the way he spoke and in the little touches they shared. While David sometimes put on a show of being annoyed, he secretly welcomed this newfound closeness.

As they chatted and had a laugh, David couldn't help but mull over how their relationship was changing. The trust and connection they'd built had turned their friendship into something deeper. But with David's missing memories and his past secrets, he was a bit unsure about revealing his true feelings.

Maybe, just maybe, there's a chance for something more.

As they stepped out into the lively streets of Central London, David felt a renewed determination. The city held their secrets, and David was ready to reclaim his lost memories.

David casually rocked the hoodie Ryan had given him. It had quickly become a favorite, and David couldn't imagine parting with it. Luckily, he had a feeling Ryan didn't mind at all.

Their journey to Embankment brought a mix of excitement and nerves for David. When Ryan suggested taking the tube, David simply agreed. The short tube ride, just twenty minutes, felt like a journey into the unknown.

Emerging from the tube station, they were engulfed by the vibrant atmosphere of Embankment. The city's lively energy flowed through the streets, a stark contrast to their usual low-key outings.

Their first stop was the Stairway to Heaven, a bar where Ryan had mentioned their friend Layla worked as a bartender.

David couldn't help but wonder what Layla would be like. Ryan had shared that she was one of his closest friends, but not remembering someone who played such a big part in his life was a frustrating aspect of his amnesia.

Entering the bar, David was taken aback by what happened next. A formidable woman, who could only be Layla, enveloped him in a bear hug. For a moment, David hesitated before returning the hug, surprised by the warmth and strength of her embrace.

Ryan, ever the friendly one, grinned at Layla. "Layla, got a quiet spot for us to chat?"

Layla released David from the hug, giving him a thoughtful once-over before nodding. "Sure thing. Follow me. Got a corner where we can talk without any nosy folks."

As they made their way through the dimly lit bar, Ryan briefed Layla on David's situation. David appreciated that Layla didn't look at him with pity but rather understanding.

Following Layla to a quieter part of the bar, David felt grateful for her willingness to help. He knew digging into the truth about that fateful night wouldn't be a walk in the park, but with friends like Layla and Ryan, he felt more determined to take it on.

They settled in a secluded corner, away from prying eyes. The dim lighting cast long shadows on the weathered wooden table. Layla motioned for them to take a seat, her expression serious.

"Alright," Layla began, her gaze fixed on David. "I know Ryan's given you some details, but I'll tell you what I remember. That night, I was doing my usual shift when you came in. You'd had a few drinks, and when your date stood you up, you decided to leave. I offered to get you a cab, but you refused. Not long after, I got a call from one of our regulars. He said he saw someone in an alley, all battered and bloody. I rushed over with a few others, and that's when we found you."

David leaned in, fully absorbed in Layla's tale, his heart pounding in his chest. Hearing about himself from someone else's point of view was strange, especially when it came to that night when his memory had been wiped clean.

Layla's voice took on a kind tone, as if she was going back to those anxious moments. "You were out cold, and there was blood everywhere—bloody scary stuff. We rang for an ambulance right away.

It was quite the ordeal, and we were all proper worried."

A flood of questions swirled in David's mind, but he knew he needed to be patient. He had to hear everything Layla had to say.

"We didn't spot anyone else around," Layla explained with a hint of frustration. "The coppers showed up, and we spilled everything we knew. But honestly, David, it was a mad night, and the leads were about as clear as mud. Just glad to see you standing here now."

David took in Layla's words, thankful for her honesty. The lack of concrete answers was maddening, but he understood that some things were destined to remain hidden.

"Thanks, Layla," David said sincerely.

Ryan chimed in, his hand offering support on David's shoulder. "Yeah, Layla, you have no idea how much we appreciate you being there that night."

Layla's tough exterior melted into a warm smile, touched by their gratitude. "You lot, it's no problem at all. If you ever need more info or if something jogs my memory, just give us a shout."

As they left the bar, David's mind was buzzing with thoughts.

Ryan sensed this and placed a comforting hand on his shoulder. "I know, mate. It's incredibly frustrating. But we'll keep digging, keep hunting down those missing pieces of the puzzle."

David nodded, grateful for Ryan's unwavering support. "Yeah, I hope so."

18

David

"SO, WHERE DO YOU WANT TO GO NEXT?" David asked Ryan as soon as they left Embankment.

Ryan grinned, his eyes sparkling mischievously. "Well, I delved into my little box of wonders that I snagged from your room and discovered your ticket for Wickd in the West End. That gave me an idea to treat you to a show today." He reached into his pocket and pulled out two tickets, handing one to David. It was a ticket to see Dreamgirl at the West End. "They were fully booked, but I managed to work some magic."

David's eyes widened with surprise. "Ryan, you didn't have to do this. It must have cost you a pretty penny."

Ryan chuckled and placed a hand on David's shoulder. "Don't fret about the cost, mate. I just want you to have a good time."

Touched by his friend's gesture, David pulled Ryan into a grateful hug. As they embraced, he felt Ryan's sigh of contentment, and Ryan held him tightly, expressing his own appreciation for their friendship.

"What time is the show?" David asked after they broke the hug.

Ryan checked his watch. "The show won't start for a couple of hours, so we've got some time to explore."

David noticed the mischievous twinkle in Ryan's eye and couldn't help but raise an eyebrow. "What's up your sleeve?"

Ryan simply grinned and motioned for David to follow him. David shook his head, amused by his friend's antics, and decided to embrace the surprise.

"When in Rome," David muttered to himself as he followed Ryan into their next adventure.

David couldn't help but grumble as Ryan led him all around central London. He complained about the endless walking and the numerous detours, but Ryan just laughed it off, clearly enjoying David's melodrama.

"Ryan, are we seriously going to explore every nook and cranny of this city?" David groaned, his voice tinged with playful exasperation.

Ryan turned around and flashed a grin at David's expense. "Mate, we're on an adventure! You can't experience London from your sofa. Plus, who knows, maybe you'll remember something if we stumble upon the right spot."

David chuckled, secretly relishing his own theatrical complaints. Being out and about in the heart of London did feel invigorating, even if his memory remained elusive.

"Alright, alright," David conceded with a dramatic eye roll. "Lead the way, tour guide."

With that, Ryan took the lead and guided them through the maze of streets until they arrived at Carnaby Street.

David's earlier grumbling turned into gasps of wonder as they turned the corner and stepped onto the cobblestone street. Overhead lights created a magical canopy, and the lively crowd bustling about filled the narrow street with vibrant energy.

"Carnaby Street," Ryan proudly announced, making a sweeping gesture. "A hidden gem right here in the heart of London. It's one of our go-to spots."

David's earlier annoyance quickly melted away as he took in the scene. It felt like they had stumbled upon a secret paradise tucked away in the city, and he couldn't help but break into a wide grin.

"Wow, this place is fantastic," David admitted, his eyes sparkling with newfound excitement.

Ryan chuckled. "That's London for you, mate. Always something new to find."

Yet, beneath the surface, David couldn't shake his frustration. Ryan had casually mentioned they used to hang out and enjoy Carnaby Street, but David couldn't remember any of it. That fact was starting to gnaw at him, fueling self-doubt.

Sensing his friend's growing unease, Ryan stepped in, determined to keep David's spirits up. He turned to David with a reassuring smile.

"Don't let it get you down, mate," Ryan comforted him. "We'll make new memories together. That's what keeps life interesting, right?"

David nodded, grateful for Ryan's support. Even if he couldn't recall past experiences, being with his best friend was a source of comfort. Determined to make the most of the moment, they continued their exploration of Carnaby Street.

They ventured into quirky shops filled with eccentric merchandise, laughing as they tried on outlandish hats and sunglasses. David may not have remembered these escapades, but the thrill of exploration and their camaraderie were something he cherished in the present.

As they roamed the vibrant street, Ryan paused in front of a street performer strumming a catchy tune on his guitar. He tossed some coins into the performer's hat, encouraging David to do the same. David happily complied, the music adding to the cheerful atmosphere of their outing.

Ice cream vendors lined the street, their colourful carts brimming with tempting flavours. Ryan didn't have to ask twice before David eagerly agreed to share a scoop of salted caramel ice cream. They savoured their treats, the sweet and salty combination a perfect match for their playful banter.

With ice cream-stained lips and laughter in their hearts, they decided to capture the moment with a series of ridiculous selfies. David couldn't resist making funny faces, while Ryan posed with exaggerated expressions. Tourists and locals alike watched with amusement as the duo's antics unfolded.

As the evening wore on, they found themselves in front of a small stage where a street magician was performing tricks that left the crowd in awe. David couldn't help but marvel at the sleight of hand and the magician's witty banter. When the magician asked for a volunteer from the audience, Ryan eagerly raised David's hand, much to his surprise.

Before he knew it, David was on stage, part of a magic act that involved disappearing scarves and floating objects. He played along with it, and when the magician finally revealed the secret behind the tricks, the entire crowd burst into applause.

David returned to Ryan's side, his cheeks flushed with both embarrassment and amusement. "I can't believe you volunteered me!"

Ryan grinned, playfully draping an arm over David's shoulder. "Come on, mate, it's all in good fun!"

Their adventure continued with more ice cream, impromptu dances to street musicians, and even a lively game of trying to spot the quirkiest shop window displays. David had to admit that despite his initial reluctance, he was having a blast rediscovering London with Ryan by his side.

They strolled along, their fingers brushing against each other, and without a second thought, David reached out to take Ryan's hand. He expected Ryan to pull away, but to his surprise, their fingers intertwined, their palms pressed together comfortably. They walked hand in hand, exploring every corner of Carnaby Street as if they had been doing it for years.

It felt natural, effortless, and David couldn't deny the warmth that enveloped him as he shared this moment with his best friend in the heart of London.

The setting sun cast a warm, golden glow over the Thames as Ryan and David found a cozy bench by the riverside. With their fingers interlocked, they watched the day's hustle and bustle give way to the serenity of twilight. The twinkling lights of the city started to paint a magical atmosphere.

"So, tell me," David began, his tone playful, "what was your absolute favourite part of our little adventure through Carnaby Street today?"

Ryan flashed a charming smile, his eyes alight with a mix of fondness and amusement. "Well, seeing you get lost in that vinyl record shop was pretty high up on the list," he admitted, his voice tinged with nostalgia. "You had this look of pure joy on your face, like a kid in a candy shop."

David chuckled, remembering the moment vividly. "I couldn't resist the allure of those classic vinyl records. And when you started humming along to that old Beatles song, I knew I had to join in."

Their laughter danced along the river's edge, their shared time together and jokes strengthening the bond they had.

As the conversation flowed, their eyes locked onto one another, their connection deepening with each passing moment. The tranquil beauty of the scene around them seemed to fade into the background, leaving only the two of them in their own private world.

Without a word, Ryan leaned in, and their lips met in a soft, tender kiss. It was as if time itself slowed down, allowing them to savor every precious second.

Memories flashed before David's eyes, like snapshots from their shared history.

They were thirteen, sitting side by side in their school uniforms, the teacher's monotonous voice fading into the background. A crumpled note passed between them, a simple invitation.

"Meet me by the old oak tree during lunch," the note read, adorned with a hastily drawn smiley face.

Under the shade of that ancient oak tree, they shared sandwiches and secrets. Ryan's laughter was infectious, and David felt drawn to the warmth in his eyes.

When their lips finally parted, David expected the usual surge of pain and confusion that accompanied his resurfacing memories. Yet, to his surprise, all he felt was an overwhelming sense of contentment. It was as though the missing pieces of his past had finally found their place.

Ryan's eyes sparkled with affection as he cupped David's face, his thumb gently caressing his cheek. "Was that alright?" he asked, his voice soft and filled with tenderness.

Unable to find the right words, David simply nodded, a warm smile curving his lips. In moments like these, words felt superfluous, for the profound connection they shared transcended mere language.

They remained seated by the Thames, hands entwined, basking in the beauty of the setting sun and the promises it held for their future adventures.

19

Ryan

DAVID AND RYAN PRACTICALLY JOGGED along the South Bank. Their laughter echoed through the crisp evening air, and passersby couldn't help but shoot them a grin at the sight of two mates clearly having a blast.

David's hand was clamped onto Ryan's, fingers interlocked like they'd been doing it for ages, even though it felt kinda new and exciting. Ryan's heart was still doing a happy dance, his mind going all over the place.

What was that kiss by the Thames about? he wondered with a chuckle in his head. It had just happened, like some kind of magical impulse triggered by all the emotions they'd bottled up over the years.

Well that answered the question if I was full-on straight, Ryan thought, his cheeks warming at the memory of David's lips on his. But it was a good kind of revelation, one he didn't mind exploring further.

However, time wasn't on their side. Ryan glanced at his watch and realised that if they didn't pick up the pace, they'd be late for the show he'd planned.

"David," he panted a bit, "we need to hustle. The West End show's gonna start soon."

David gave a quick nod, still a bit flushed from their laughter and the chilly breeze from the river. "Right, let's get a move on. Can't wait to see what you've got in store for us."

They picked up the pace, fingers still entwined, and made a beeline for the Prince Edward Theatre. Ryan had managed to nab seats close to the front, and the look on David's face when he saw their spots was absolutely priceless.

"You're a legend, Ryan."

Ryan couldn't help but flash a grin. "Only the best for you, mate."

Once they settled into their seats, Ryan decided to keep the hand-holding thing going. David shot him a warm smile and squeezed his hand in return, and together, they turned their attention to the stage.

The performance of Dreamgirls was absolutely mind-blowing. The actors' voices filled the theatre, spinning a captivating tale of dreams, love, and ambition. David and Ryan shared hearty laughs at the funny bits and had to discreetly wipe away a tear or two during the emotional numbers. It was a rollercoaster of feels, and they loved every minute of it.

During one particularly touching scene, David brushed away a sneaky tear that dared to escape. Ryan, overcome with affection for his mate, leaned closer and whispered, "Nothing wrong with shedding a tear, you know. This show gets me every time."

David let out a soft chuckle, his gaze still glued to the stage. "I can see why. It's incredible."

As the final curtain fell, the audience burst into applause. David turned to Ryan, his eyes filled with gratitude. "Thanks for this, Ryan. It's been unforgettable."

Ryan's heart swelled with happiness, knowing he'd hit the bullseye with this surprise. "You're welcome, David. So glad you enjoyed it."

After the show, they walked out onto the bustling London streets. Ryan hailed an Uber, and they hopped into the back seat, still riding the high from the performance.

David leaned back, shooting Ryan a grin. "You know, today's been bloody amazing. From Carnaby Street to the West End, it's been a day of surprises."

Ryan nodded, his mind drifting back to that kiss by the Thames. "Yeah, it really has."

The ride back to David's place was filled with laughter and reminiscing about the day's highlights. They chatted about their favorite moments from the show, and David couldn't stop raving about the ice cream they'd scarfed down earlier.

As they pulled up in front of David's flat, he turned to Ryan. "Thanks, mate, not just for today, but for being there for me through all of this."

Ryan grinned, feeling the warmth of their friendship. "David, no need for thanks. We're in this together, whatever comes our way."

They both knew the journey to unlock David's lost memories was far from over. But in that moment, they found comfort in each other's company.

As soon as they walked into the flat, David leaned in, and without a moment's hesitation, Ryan met him halfway for a sweet, lingering kiss.

As their clothes started coming off, David and Ryan made their way to the bed. They playfully undressed each other, their touches and glances teasing and building anticipation. Their desire grew as they neared the bed.

On the bed, they continued exploring each other's bodies, taking turns pleasuring one another. This was Ryan's first time engaging with a guy, and he couldn't wait to explore more.

"Ryan… Ryan… wait," David said, and Ryan paused, his actions frozen. David's words hung in the air, and Ryan felt a pang of guilt. He hadn't intended to rush things, especially given David's amnesia, but his overwhelming feelings had carried him away.

Ryan stopped and looked at David with concern. "Why? What's wrong? Don't you like it?"

David's response was gentle, understanding. "I do, I really do. But don't you think it's too fast? I mean, we just kissed."

Ryan paused, reflecting on David's words. It was a moment of clarity amid the whirlwind of emotions. "I'm sorry. I don't know what got into me."

Cupping Ryan's cheeks, David reassured him, "Hey, none of that, okay? You're new to all of this, and considering my situation, I'm sort of new to it too."

Ryan moved closer, seeking warmth and comfort in David's embrace. David's presence felt right, his scent soothing Ryan's racing thoughts. "I thought I was straight for the longest time," Ryan admitted quietly.

David's fingers traced soothing patterns on Ryan's arms as he probed further. "What changed? And are you saying that I wasn't like that when I still had my memory?"

Ryan chose his words carefully. "I didn't say that, but yeah, you always kept me at arm's length when it came to being physical. But there were things that I found out that made me understand the reason why."

Curiosity and a hint of concern filled David's eyes. "What aren't you telling me, Ryan?" he asked gently.

Ryan took a deep breath before continuing. "Remember when you found me in your room at your parents' house?" David nodded. "Well, I found these letters under your bed."

"Letters?"

Ryan nodded, his fingers still caressing David's stomach. "Yeah, they were letters that you wrote but never sent."

David's brow furrowed as he processed this information. "Who were they meant to go to?"

"To me," Ryan admitted, his voice barely above a whisper. "After reading them, everything made more sense. That got me thinking, and that's when I realized that I was blinded by my own desire to have a family that I never thought about exploring my sexuality."

David took a moment to absorb this revelation before posing another question. "And now? What do you want?"

Ryan met David's gaze directly. "It's not about what I want anymore. It's about who I want. And that person is you. I'm so sorry if it took me this long to figure things out."

Tears welled up in Ryan's eyes, and he hadn't even noticed until David tenderly wiped them away. "Ryan, there's no timeframe when it comes to figuring out your sexuality. Even my damaged brain knew that. What matters now is that you finally found yourself."

"Your brain isn't damaged, David. Please remember that," Ryan whispered, his voice filled with love and acceptance, as he cupped David's face and kissed him.

Their lips met in a sweet, passionate kiss, sealing their newfound understanding and affection. It was a kiss that spoke of forgiveness, acceptance, and a promise of a deeper connection.

After their intimate moment, David expressed his curiosity about the letters. "Can I see one of these letters?"

"Sure, stay here," Ryan said, a smile on his face as he got up and retrieved one of the letters from the living room.

Ryan returned with the letter in hand, and David took it gently. The paper felt slightly worn, as if it had been read and reread many times. He opened the envelope with care, revealing handwritten words that held the secrets of his past and the key to his heart.

The letter spoke of David's internal struggles, his fear of judgment, and his longing for acceptance. It was a heartfelt confession of feelings that had remained unspoken for far too long.

Ryan watched David's reaction with a mix of anticipation and vulnerability, waiting for his response to the words that had laid bare his innermost thoughts and feelings.

With the letter in hand, David finally looked up at Ryan, his eyes filled with tenderness and understanding. "Thank you for sharing this with me," he said softly.

"I should be thanking you," Ryan said as he took the letter from David. He folded it neatly and placed it on the nightstand next to him before kissing David's forehead. "Come on, let's go to sleep." David nodded, and they cuddled together.

Ryan stayed awake for a little longer, staring up at the ceiling and thinking about what he had to do next. One thing was for sure: he needed to finish things off with Elle.

He sighed and snuggled up with David before he could lose his mind over it.

20

Ryan

RYAN, WEARING AN APRON, stood by the stove, flipping bacon in a sizzling pan and cracking eggs into another. The kitchen was filled with the delicious smell of breakfast cooking.

As he hummed a tune to himself, Ryan felt strong arms wrap around him from behind. David's embrace was both comforting and electrifying, making Ryan pause and let out a contented sigh.

"You're a lovely sight in the morning," David said, nuzzling Ryan's neck.

Ryan smiled, feeling David's warmth against his back. "Morning. I'm making us some eggs and bacon."

David peered over Ryan's shoulder at the sizzling pan. "Ah, the classic English breakfast. Good choice."

Sitting at the kitchen table with their plates piled high with eggs and bacon, Ryan knew he had to talk to David about Elle before things got complicated.

"Something on your mind, Ryan?" David asked, sounding concerned.

Ryan sighed and put down his fork. He couldn't keep this secret any longer. "David, there's something I need to tell you."

David looked at him attentively. "Go on, I'm all ears."

Taking a deep breath, Ryan began, "I have a girlfriend, her name's Elle."

David furrowed his brow, trying to recall the name. "Elle? I don't think I know her."

"Yeah, you introduced us at a party once," Ryan admitted, feeling a bit embarrassed. "And things kind of started from there."

David's expression softened as he covered Ryan's hand with his own. "You should have told me sooner, Ryan."

Ryan glanced down at his plate, his appetite disappearing. "I know, I should have, but things got complicated, and I didn't want to overwhelm you."

David squeezed Ryan's hand gently. "It's okay, you can talk about it now."

Ryan met David's eyes. "The truth is, David, I want to be with you. I want us to be together."

The room fell silent as David absorbed Ryan's confession, the unspoken emotions between them palpable.

Finally, David spoke, his voice filled with empathy. "And Elle?"

Ryan sighed, his shoulders slumping. "I'm done with Elle. It's not fair to her, and it's not fair to us. I don't love her the way I should."

David nodded slowly, never breaking eye contact. "Are you sure about this, Ryan? Ending things with her?"

Ryan met David's gaze with determination. "I'm sure. It's time to move forward."

David reached out and placed a comforting hand on Ryan's. "I just don't want you to rush into anything, especially because of me."

Ryan smiled, his affection for David shining through. "I've thought about this for a while, and I think it's the right thing to do."

Finishing breakfast, Ryan felt a shift inside him. Today marked a new chapter, and he was ready to tackle the tough task ahead with David's support.

After tidying up, they headed to David's parents' place. Holding hands felt natural, though facing David's parents as a couple brought nerves and excitement. They shared a reassuring glance that melted away some of the anxiety.

David's parents greeted them with warm smiles, their eyes resting on their intertwined hands. Ryan led David inside, feeling their unspoken approval. As he promised to return later, he gave David a tender kiss, witnessed by his approving parents.

Alone now, Ryan sent a quick text to Elle, asking to meet at a Costa in Ealing Broadway.

In the quiet coffee shop, Ryan sat at a corner table with a latte, watching the entrance. When Elle arrived, determined and focused, he waved her over.

Elle didn't waste time with pleasantries, her expression skeptical. "What's going on, Ryan? You've been acting strange lately."

Taking a deep breath, Ryan prepared himself. "Elle, this isn't easy, but it's time for us to break up."

Elle's eyes widened in surprise, quickly turning to frustration. "What are you talking about? Is this some sort of joke?"

Ryan shook his head, his tone serious but composed. "No joke, Elle. I've thought about it, and it's the best choice for both of us."

Elle's frustration grew, her voice tinged with bitterness. "Is there someone else, Ryan? Is that why you're doing this?"

Ryan paused, selecting his words carefully. "It's not about someone else, Elle. It's about us. My feelings have changed, and I won't pretend."

Elle's anger flared, her voice low but intense. "So, you're just ending this, after everything we've been through?"

Ryan sighed. "I don't want to hurt you, Elle. I just think it's time for us to move forward."

Elle's frustration boiled over, and she slammed her hand on the table.

"Who's taken you from me, Ryan?"

Ryan remained composed, keeping the truth about David hidden. "No one, Elle. This is about what I need right now."

Tears welled up in Elle's eyes, her voice shaking. "You'll regret this, Ryan."

As Elle stormed out of the coffee shop, Ryan felt the weight of their shared history. Ending things was right, but it didn't make it easier.

Sipping his coffee, he contemplated the future ahead, filled with the promise of a fresh start with David. Challenges awaited, but they were ready to face them together.

21

David

"HEY, SON, HOW IS IT GOING?" David's Dad asked, striking up a conversation.

David tried to sound cheerful as he replied, "I'm hanging in there."

Honestly, he's a bit fed up with feeling frustrated all the time, but he didn't want to dump all of his worries on his folks.

"And what about Ryan?" His Mum asked.

David thought about the brave conversations he'd had with Ryan last night and that morning. A mix of feelings swirled within him—gratitude, a touch of anxiety, and a bunch of 'what ifs' that kept popping up. But for now, he didn't want to dwell on them.

"Ryan's doing alright, more or less," David replied to his Mum.

"Did something finally happen between you two?" His Dad, grinning cheekily, asked.

"Lucas!" His Mum scolded her husband but David just chuckled.

Rubbing the back of his neck, David wondered how much he should share with his parents. "There's not much to say. What we've got going on is pretty new."

His Dad playfully jabbed at Ryan, saying, "It's about time. That lad really needed to pull his head out of his rear end."

"Lucas! Lay off Ryan. We're thrilled for you, David. You've had a thing for him forever," His Mum said, giving him a tight hug.

David felt genuinely touched by his parents' support. "What's been happening with you guys? How's everything here?"

"Oh, we're doing alright. The bakery's still a hit," his Mum replied.

"Bakery?" David perked up at that.

His parents exchanged knowing glances before chuckling. "Yeah, dear. It's the bakery you helped us set up. If it weren't for you, we wouldn't have given it a shot," David's Dad explained.

"Can I drop by sometime?" David inquired.

"Absolutely, love. How about coming over tomorrow and bringing Ryan along?" his Mum suggested, sealing the deal with a warm smile.

After a while, David's Dad took him into the kitchen and tossed him an apron. His Dad had this mischievous twinkle in his eye. "David, my lad, how about learning the art of baking like a proper bloke?"

David chuckled at his Dad's unexpected idea. "Dad, you've got yourself a baking apprentice. Let's see if I've got what it takes to whip up some tasty treats."

Their spontaneous baking adventure kicked off with a bang. Flour was flying everywhere as they got into a friendly flour toss, ending up looking like something out of a comedy show. Laughter filled the air, making the whole scene feel joyous.

Meanwhile, David's Mum sat at the dining table, watching the floury battlefield with a fond smile.

With aprons on, they got down to the real deal of baking. His Dad generously shared family recipes and baking tricks, guiding David through it all with a mix of patience and good humor. The kitchen soon smelled divine with cookies in the making.

Once they'd expertly shaped the cookie dough and prepped the trays for the oven, they cranked up the heat and set the timer. With some time to spare before their sweet creations were ready, they joined his Mum at the dining table.

Sipping hot tea and nibbling on homemade biscuits his Mum had made earlier, they relished the simple pleasure of being together as a family.

"So, any progress with your memories, love?" His Mum asked.

David thought for a moment about how much to share, knowing that memories could be a delicate thing. Eventually, he decided to give them a glimpse of what he'd been going through. "Well, some memories have been coming back."

"Can you tell us more?" His Mum asked softly, reaching out to give David's hand a reassuring squeeze.

David hesitated for a second but then decided to open up a bit more. "I've been remembering moments with Ryan."

"Ryan, eh? Does he know about all this?" His Dad asked.

David shook his head, emotions swirling inside him. "No, he doesn't. And I reckon it's about time I have a chat with him about it."

His Mum leaned in, giving David a warm, supportive hug. "Whatever you decide, David, we're here for you."

Lucas chimed in with a grin, "And we'll be here, eagerly waiting to taste the results of your baking experiments."

His parents' support was like a reassuring anchor in the ever-changing whirlwind of his memories and feelings.

"So, what do you guys remember about me and Ryan?" David asked, his eyes shifting between his Mum and Dad, hoping their recollections could fill in his own gaps.

His Mum leaned back in her chair, looking thoughtful. "Well, love, you two crossed paths when you were just thirteen, and he's been a big part of your life ever since."

His Dad chimed in with a grin, "Ryan's a top bloke, he is. He's been like a second son to us."

David's heart swelled with warmth at their words. He really wanted to piece together his scattered memories and understand the role Ryan had played in his life and his heart.

Just as David was lost in thought, the front door creaked open, and Ryan walked in. His usually lively eyes seemed a bit tired, but they brightened up when he saw David. He offered a tired but genuine smile, and David's heart did a little dance at the sight of him.

"Hey," David greeted Ryan.

Ryan's eyes softened as he came closer. "Hey to you too."

He wrapped his arms around David, pulling him into a snug hug. They shared a moment of wordless comfort, and David could feel Ryan's heartbeat against his chest.

David gestured for Ryan to join them at the dining room table. As Ryan settled into a chair, his Dad couldn't help but be direct.

"Ryan, lad, how did things go with… you know, 'that woman'?" His Dad asked, curiosity twinkling in his eyes.

Ryan let out a relieved sigh, the tension from his earlier chat with Elle fading away. "It's all sorted, Lucas. Finally."

David's heart swelled with gratitude as he looked at Ryan. He knew how much courage it took for Ryan to end things with Elle for their sake.

David's Dad, however, didn't hold back. "Good riddance, I say. She wasn't the one for you, mate."

His Mum nodded in agreement. "We never really felt the love between you two, Ryan. You deserve someone who truly makes your heart sing."

Ryan blushed a bit, touched by their words. "Your support means the world to me."

As they carried on chatting, David couldn't help but think about the incredible people in his life. His parents, always there with love and support, and Ryan, the missing piece of his complicated puzzle.

Around that dining room table, they were a family, bound together by love and acceptance.

They continued talking and laughing for a couple more hours, the cozy atmosphere of David's parents' home embracing them like a warm blanket. But eventually, David began to feel the weight of exhaustion tugging at his eyelids.

Ryan, being the caring partner he is, noticed David looking a bit tired. "Fancy heading back home?" he asked, a warm smile on his face.

David nodded, showing his fatigue. "I reckon I'm ready."

"Alright, then," Ryan turned to his parents, gratitude in his eyes. "Thanks for looking after him today. It means a lot."

His Mum beamed. "Our pleasure, dear. And don't forget, David wanted to visit the bakery with us tomorrow. You're more than welcome to join."

Ryan agreed. "Sounds good. Just remember to stock up on those protein cookies I can't resist."

Lucas chuckled and nodded. "Consider it sorted. Now, you two best be off before it gets too late."

With heartfelt hugs and parting words, David and Ryan found themselves outside, the evening air getting a bit chilly. Ryan looked at David, and his hand reached out to hold David's.

"Wanna head home?" Ryan asked, his voice gentle and caring.

David met Ryan's gaze and teased, "What's going on in that Evans brain of yours?" A mischievous grin played on his lips.

Ryan cleared his throat, determination in his eyes. "I was thinking of taking you on a proper date."

David couldn't resist teasing Ryan a bit more, their affection for each other clear. "Well, Mr. Evans, you do know how to persuade me."

Closing the gap between them, Ryan planted a sweet kiss on David's lips. It felt like the world around them lit up in that moment. When they pulled away, Ryan wore a proud grin.

"How was that?" he asked, his voice tender.

David chuckled, his heart full of affection. "You, Mr. Evans, are quite the charmer. Lead the way."

Hand in hand, they walked through the dimly lit streets, their path brightened by the promise of a romantic date.

Piccadilly Circus was alive with its flashy lights and bustling energy. Ryan and David stepped out of the Underground station into the heart of the city, surrounded by towering billboards and the hustle and bustle of Londoners and tourists.

Ryan's choice for their next stop was a bit unexpected – M&M's World. David's eyes lit up like a kid's on Christmas morning as they entered the candy wonderland. The sight and smell of chocolate overwhelmed him, and he couldn't contain his excitement.

Ryan couldn't help but laugh at David's pure joy. "You're seriously like a kid in a candy store," he teased, grinning.

David shot back with a grin of his own. "Well, technically, we are in a candy store, aren't we?"

David grabbed a bunch of M&M's goodies, including keychains, plush toys, and, of course, bags of M&M's in every shade under the sun.

They lost track of time wandering through the store, immersing themselves in the world of chocolates. David was on a sugar high, and he was loving every second of it.

When they finally left M&M's World with bags filled with colorful sweets, David's candy craving was temporarily satisfied. They decided to take a leisurely walk to Leicester Square.

Ryan led David to a seemingly ordinary entrance that opened up to a wine bar tucked beneath the bustling square. David was pleasantly surprised by the cozy, well-lit atmosphere. It had a charming vibe with its classy lighting and comfy seating.

Once they settled into a quiet corner, David couldn't contain his excitement any longer. He took a sip of his wine, leaned closer to Ryan, and grinned.

"Hey, something pretty cool happened a couple of days ago," David began.

Ryan leaned in, intrigued. "What's up?"

David chuckled before spilling the beans. "I remembered something about us, about when we first met."

Ryan's eyebrows shot up in surprise. "Really? That's amazing! What did you remember?"

David's face lit up with nostalgia. "Well, I recalled our first encounter in school. You were the new kid, and me being the nosy guy I am, I decided to introduce myself. Little did I know, that moment would shape our entire friendship."

Ryan chuckled, a fond smile on his lips. "I remember that day too. I was so nervous, but when you reached out, it felt like a lifeline in a sea of strangers."

David met Ryan's gaze, his voice soft. "I felt safe, Ryan. Like I'd stumbled upon something incredibly precious."

Ryan's fingers brushed David's cheek gently as their foreheads touched. "And how do you feel now that these memories are coming back?"

David's heart swelled, and he couldn't help but smile. "I feel like I'm piecing together a part of myself that I thought was lost. And I'm grateful that you've been a part of my life, Ryan."

Ryan's hand cupped David's face tenderly as their foreheads touched. "I'm grateful too, David. Grateful for every moment we've shared and for all the moments we're yet to create."

Their intimate conversation in the cozy wine bar felt like a beautiful connection. Memories from the past were resurfacing, strengthening their bond and opening up new possibilities for their future.

They then talked about Elle and the recent breakup. David couldn't help but voice his concern.

"Are you sure Elle won't cause any trouble?" he asked, worry creasing his brow.

Ryan reached across the table, their fingers intertwining. "I promise, David, everything's under control. She knows it's over."

David's smile held a sense of relief as he squeezed Ryan's hand. Their connection felt stronger, and a wave of warmth washed over him.

Hours flew by as they savored each other's company. Every word, every glance, every shared laugh deepened their bond.

Leaving the wine bar, the moonlight cast a soft glow over Leicester Square. David couldn't help but feel grateful for this extraordinary day.

Walking hand in hand through the city streets, hearts brimming with joy and excitement for the future, they knew this was just the beginning of their journey together.

22

Ryan

T HE COZY LITTLE BAKERY, SugarBliss, was a sweet escape filled with the mouthwatering smell of freshly baked goodies. The morning had a crisp edge to it, promising the warmth of pastries and cookies. It was impossible not to smile.

David had been buzzing with excitement about this bakery visit since they rolled out of bed this morning, and it was infectious. Last night, they'd all snuggled up in the same bed – even Tyson had joined in at some point.

Ryan couldn't resist leaning in for a soft kiss on David's lips. Together, hand in hand, they pushed open the bakery door, making the little bell hanging above jingle cheerfully as if it welcomed them personally.

Inside, the place was bustling with life, a testament to David's parents' thriving business. Irene spotted them and waved them over to a cozy corner adorned with rustic wooden furniture and warm colors that gave off a snug vibe. A friendly staff member named Jane promptly appeared with two steaming cups of tea and served them with a warm smile.

"Morning, you two," Irene greeted them, wiping her flour-covered hands on her apron, leaving powdery streaks as she did so.

"Morning, Mum," David replied, his eyes already locked onto the spread of heavenly baked treats.

In the busy kitchen, Irene and Lucas orchestrated a symphony of ovens, mixers, and dough, expertly crafting their renowned pastries. The sounds of clinking utensils and the gentle hum of the ovens created a comforting background melody.

Ryan couldn't help leaning in closer to David, mischief lighting up his eyes as he whispered, "Hope you've got your appetite ready for your folks' legendary pastries."

David chuckled, still fixated on the mouthwatering choices. "Wouldn't miss it for the world. They've created something truly special here."

Jane returned with a tray overflowing with flaky croissants, gooey cinnamon rolls, and a variety of muffins. Even in the middle of their bustling bakery, Irene and Lucas made sure their guests felt like part of the family.

Amid bites of delicious treats and sips of tea, their corner of SugarBliss filled with laughter and warmth. David's parents had turned their bakery into a home away from home, evident in the smiles and greetings exchanged with regular customers who seemed more like old pals.

As time rolled on, Irene and Lucas pulled up chairs at their table, their hands covered in flour, and rosy cheeks hinting at the heat from the ovens. David couldn't hold back his excitement, launching into tales of their baking adventures from the previous day, while Ryan sprinkled in his playful remarks.

Lucas looked at his son with pride, his eyes twinkling. "David, you've always had a talent for baking. It's in your blood, you know."

David's grin could have lit up the room. "It's incredible to see what you both have accomplished here."

Irene leaned in, wrapping David in a warm hug. "We're thrilled to have you and Ryan as a part of this."

SugarBliss meant more than just a bakery; it was a place where hearts were nourished, and where love was baked into every treat.

With warm smiles, David's parents returned to the kitchen to attend to the growing crowd of customers, leaving David and Ryan to enjoy their meal. But David had a different idea.

"Hey, how about we lend them a hand while we're here?" David suggested, taking Ryan by delightful surprise.

"Really?" Ryan grinned and didn't think twice about slipping his hand under the table to hold David's. "Count me in."

They both stood up, their excitement clear as day, and headed towards the bustling kitchen where Irene and Lucas orchestrated the delightful chaos.

"What brings you two back here?" Irene asked, her smile never wavering.

Ryan chimed in eagerly, "David thought we could help out, so hand over those aprons and let's get to work."

Lucas tossed them aprons, and they quickly donned the baker-in-training attire. Lucas directed their roles, saying, "David, you're with me. Ryan, you can take care of serving. Is that alright?"

"Absolutely," Ryan agreed with enthusiasm. Before venturing to the front of the bakery, he exchanged a quick, reassuring glance with David. "Are you going to be okay here?"

David nodded, leaning in for a comforting kiss. "Yeah, go ahead. I'll be just fine."

As Ryan joined the hustle and bustle at the front of the bakery, he effortlessly slipped into the rhythm. Taking orders, manning the cash register, and ensuring each customer left with a smile felt like second nature. The atmosphere was buzzing, filled with lively conversations and shared laughter.

As Ryan occasionally glanced back towards the kitchen, he

caught glimpses of David and Lucas working side by side. It was heartwarming—the passing down of traditions, those smiles brimming with pride, and the bonding over labor. The kitchen wasn't just a place for expertise; it was filled with love and learning.

David's hands expertly handled the dough, his face beaming with satisfaction. Lucas, his father, nodded approvingly, sharing more than just baking tips—it was life wisdom. Ryan and David, with their subtle looks and knowing smiles, communicated their shared joy and sense of belonging without uttering a word.

After the final batch of pastries was out of the ovens, David and Ryan took a well-deserved break. They sat at a corner table, sipping tea and nibbling on freshly baked scones. Flour was their badge of honor, and their smiles spoke of contentment.

David leaned in, his eyes locking with Ryan's. "Baking with Dad like this is a blast."

Ryan's heart swelled with affection as he squeezed David's hand gently. "I can tell. And I must say, this apron isn't half bad."

David chuckled, his fingers entwined with Ryan's. "You do look rather cute in it."

Playfully teasing, Ryan shot back, "I couldn't let you have all the baking fun, could I?"

Their scones were savored, and their joy was in the simple act of being together.

As the day turned into evening, Irene and Lucas thanked them warmly for their help and insisted they take home a box of their favorite pastries.

"Where to now?" Ryan asked as they strolled through the lively streets of London.

David thought for a moment. "I was thinking of heading home and maybe reading some of the letters," he replied with a soft smile.

Ryan studied David, a hint of concern in his eyes. "Are you sure?" he asked, his protective instincts surfacing.

David teased, "Yeah, unless you've got some secret plans you're not telling me?" He caught Ryan off guard with a playful quip.

Ryan hadn't made secret plans yet, but he remembered that David's birthday was approaching, and he needed to start planning.

Thinking on his feet, Ryan suggested, "We could grab some takeout on the way back to your place."

But David surprised Ryan with his response. "It's your home now, too, Ryan. Actually, I wouldn't mind if you moved in completely."

Ryan was momentarily stunned, overwhelmed by David's willingness to embrace him fully, despite the challenges they faced. Without words, he expressed his feelings by leaning in for a passionate, lingering kiss. Everything around them faded, leaving only the two of them and the promise of a shared future.

Breathless and lost in the moment, they finally pulled away, foreheads touching. "Yes, I'll move in with you," Ryan whispered.

Their tender moment was interrupted by cheers and applause from nearby. David's parents were watching, tears of joy in their eyes. A nod of approval from Irene and Lucas sealed the deal.

Ryan and David shared a chuckle, hearts warmed by the support of their loved ones. They hugged tightly, reaffirming their commitment to each other, before continuing their journey home.

23

Ryan

THE TUBE JOURNEY BACK TO KNIGHTSBRIDGE was a mix of chatter and contentment. Ryan and David settled into the subway seats, the gentle sway of the train lulling them into a state of relaxation.

Ryan had that mischievous twinkle in his eye as he pulled David towards a Thai restaurant they'd grown to love. The scent of spices and flavours enveloped them as they stepped inside, and the cozy atmosphere seemed to say, "Welcome home."

David couldn't resist asking the obvious question, a playful smile tugging at his lips. "So, what's the deal with this place, Ry?"

Ryan let out a chuckle, his fingers drumming lightly on the laminated menu. "Well, apart from the fact that it's budget-friendly, it's perfect for winding down after a day like today."

David arched an eyebrow. "Only that?"

"Nah, it's also 'cause I've got the best company in town."

They ordered their takeaways. The aromatic bags in hand, they left the restaurant, the cool summer London breeze rustling their hair as they strolled through the bustling streets.

As they approached David's building, Ryan couldn't help but reflect on the recent turn of events. David had asked him to move in, and the idea warmed Ryan's heart.

Ryan couldn't contain his disbelief as he turned to David. "You know, I'm still wrapping my head around the fact that you asked me to move in with you."

David smiled, his eyes reflecting his emotions. "I just wanted you to be a part of my everyday life, Ryan. It felt right."

As they entered their home, a sense of contentment settled over Ryan, and he couldn't help but smile at the thought.

I don't think that'll get old anytime soon, he mused to himself.

Beneath his feet, Tyson, voiced his impatience, demanding attention with persistent meowing. Ryan chuckled at the furry little creature's antics.

In the bedroom, Ryan saw that David began changing, and Ryan, momentarily lost in thought, nearly tripped over the counter. He found himself admiring his boyfriend's physique.

Boyfriend, huh? You haven't asked yet, Ryan thought, acknowledging that it was a conversation he needed to initiate soon.

David's laughter from across the room brought Ryan back to the present. "You better feed him or he'll end up pissing on your shoes later," David teased, his words snapping Ryan out of his reverie.

Ryan chuckled, responding, "Yeah, yeah. Come here, you little adorable menace."

With affectionate exasperation, Ryan picked up Tyson from the floor and headed over to the spot where they kept the cat food. Tyson had been attempting to open the bag with his claws, but Ryan's strength prevailed. After serving Tyson's dinner, Ryan joined David on the couch. To his amusement, David was already comfortably seated with his own meal.

Shaking his head in playful disbelief, Ryan settled in beside David. Their TV was tuned in to a drag queen competition on Netflix, and as they watched, they shared quiet moments punctuated by shared laughter at the show's amusing antics. For Ryan, it was pure bliss, and he couldn't have asked for a more perfect evening.

An hour later, as the show concluded, Ryan collected their dirty plates and took them to the kitchen. Returning to the living room with the box of memories in hand, he rejoined David, who was once again seated on the couch with Tyson nestled contentedly on his lap.

Curiosity piqued, David asked, "What else is in the box?"

Ryan began to explain, "Well, most of these are photos, videos, and mementos that I knew meant a lot to you."

However, as he rummaged through the box, Ryan discovered something he hadn't seen before—a pen drive with his name on it.

"What's that?"

"I don't know. This is also my first time seeing it," Ryan admitted. Intrigued, he stood up, plugged the drive into the TV, and took hold of the remote. Returning to the couch and David's side, he navigated to the folder labeled "Ryan" and selected a video file.

The TV screen flickered to life, and Ryan's heart skipped a beat as the video began to play.

The video begins with a burst of joyful laughter and the sound of snow crunching underfoot. The camera shakes slightly, revealing that it's held by David. He points it at a figure in the distance, approaching at a brisk pace.

David began narrating. "There he is, the man of the hour—Ryan."

Ryan, bundled up in a warm winter coat and a playful grin on his face, comes into view. He waves at the camera with mittened hands, his breath visible in the crisp, snowy air.

"It's our winter getaway, and I couldn't think of a better way to capture the moment."

The scene transitions to a series of shots capturing Ryan's various antics. He throws a snowball at the camera, causing a playful squeal from David.

Then, he pretends to slip on a patch of ice, earning hearty laughter from both of them.

"It's moments like these, the ones where he's just himself, that I treasure the most."

The camera switches to a close-up of Ryan's face, capturing the rosy glow of his cheeks and the sparkling mischief in his eyes.

"I mean, look at that face. How could I not fall for it?"

The video takes a poignant turn as it shows Ryan in more introspective moments. He gazes out at a snow-covered landscape, a thoughtful expression on his face.

"But there's more to him than just the laughter and the fun. He has this incredible depth, an inner strength that I admire so much."

Ryan's fingers trace patterns on a frost-covered window, and his reflection is cast against the wintry backdrop.

"He's not afraid to be vulnerable, to share his dreams and fears. And that's what makes him so incredibly special."

The video transitions to a montage of shared experiences—cozy nights by the fireplace, cups of hot cocoa, and playful snowball fights.

"We've built a world together, a world filled with love, laughter, and endless adventures."

Ryan and David stand side by side, their fingers intertwined as they watch the sun setting over a snowy horizon.

"And now, my love, if you're watching this, I want you to know that this is how I see you. The man who's brought so much joy into my life."

David's face appears on the screen, and he smiles warmly.

"And who knows, by the time you find this, we might be married or, at the very least, planning our next big adventure together." He chuckles softly.

The video ends with a lingering shot of the winter landscape, bathed in the soft glow of the setting sun.

The room felt heavy, and Ryan could sense David's emotions as they watched the video together. As the footage faded to black, he could hear David's soft, uneven breathing. They sat side by side on the couch, Ryan's arm draped around David's shoulders, providing silent support.

David's eyes glistened with unshed tears, and Ryan couldn't help but feel his own emotions welling up. The video had stirred a whirlwind of memories and emotions, now distant and elusive.

"I just… I can't remember any of it, Ryan," David finally spoke, his voice quivering with a mix of sadness and frustration. "It's like it's all gone, and I can't reach it, no matter how hard I try."

Ryan sighed, his heart aching for David. "I know," he murmured, his voice filled with empathy. He gave David's shoulder a reassuring squeeze. "I can't even begin to imagine how tough this must be for you."

David turned to him, his tearful eyes meeting Ryan's. "I'm sorry, Ryan. I'm so sorry that I can't remember all those moments we shared. It's like I'm letting you down."

Ryan shook his head firmly, his own eyes moist. "You're not letting me down, David. Not in the slightest. This memory loss, it's not your fault. It's just a damn cruel twist of fate."

David let out a shaky breath, his shoulders slumping in defeat. "I just wish I could remember. I wish I could hold on to those moments, to the way you see me in that video."

Ryan turned to David, meeting his gaze with unwavering determination. "You don't need memories to know how I see you, David. You're incredible. You're the strongest person I know. That video was just a snapshot of what we've shared. But even without those memories, I know who you are, David and nothing's going to change."

David's lower lip quivered, and he leaned into Ryan's embrace, seeking comfort. "I'm so damn grateful for you, for being here with me through all of this."

Ryan planted a tender kiss on David's head, holding him close. "We'll tackle this together, David. No matter what."

They remained in each other's arms, the quiet of the room enveloping them. The video may have brought pain, but it had also reaffirmed the depth of their feelings.

24

David

H E WAS ALONE IN BED, prompting a moment of confusion. However, a folded piece of paper on the bedside table caught his attention, and the initial bewilderment gave way to a grin as he picked it up.

Ryan's handwriting graced the page, a testament to his thoughtfulness.

David,

I hope you slept well. I'm really sorry to have left, work called. Tyson has been fed, and I've made some breakfast for you. It's in the kitchen. Please help yourself.

Take care and have a great day.

Ryan

Ryan's sweet gestures never failed to warm David's heart. Despite his absence, Ryan had gone the extra mile to ensure David would start the day with a smile, ensuring both Tyson and breakfast were well taken care of.

With a contented sigh, David decided to heed Ryan's note. After a refreshing shower and a quick change into comfortable attire, he made his way to the kitchen. The routine of getting ready for the day had become a familiar and comforting ritual. Independence was his goal, and each day brought him closer to it.

The kitchen welcomed him with the inviting aroma of breakfast, skilfully prepared by Ryan. Scrambled eggs, crispy bacon, and perfectly toasted bread adorned the table, a testament to Ryan's culinary prowess.

David savoured each bite, his mind wandering to how he'd spend the day. The idea of solitude held no intimidation; rather, it fuelled his determination to regain his independence. He knew he couldn't rely on Ryan indefinitely, and today presented another opportunity to prove to himself that he could navigate the world on his terms.

David efficiently cleaned up the dishes, leaving the kitchen as immaculate as he'd found it.

Stepping outside, he was greeted by the gentle caress of the morning breeze and the harmonious sounds of life unfurling around him. Birds sang merrily in the trees, and people exchanged cheerful greetings as they went about their routines.

The charming boutiques that lined the streets beckoned to him, inviting exploration. David had no specific destination in mind, only a desire to immerse himself in the world beyond the confines of their home.

As he meandered, David revelled in the simple yet profound beauty of life unfolding around him. Laughter echoed from a nearby park where children played, and diligent shopkeepers bustled about, tending to their businesses. The enticing scent of freshly brewed coffee wafted from a nearby cafe, adding to the sensory symphony of the day.

The vibrant energy of the city and the friendly interactions with strangers filled David with a sense of accomplishment. He'd come a long way since that day.

David casually strolled through the familiar streets of Knightsbridge, enjoying the peaceful vibes. The idea of sipping a warm cup of coffee beckoned him, and he decided to head to a nearby coffee shop.

However, as he approached the cozy cafe, a sinking feeling settled in. He realised that he still didn't have any money with him, a situation he planned to remedy by discussing the Detective's findings about his missing phone and wallet with Ryan.

Contemplating a return home, David collided with someone, momentarily startling him. He glanced up to see a woman before him. She sported striking blonde hair meticulously styled, and her makeup was Hollywood-worthy. Despite her glamorous appearance, her bright blue eyes held a genuine sense of surprise and concern.

The woman's voice rang friendly as she spoke, "Oh, I'm so sorry."

David, still slightly flustered, managed a reassuring smile. "No worries, it was my fault."

Her warm demeanour was a stark contrast to her glamorous look. "Are you here alone?" she asked.

David hesitated, unsure of how much he wanted to divulge to a stranger about his situation. "Um, yeah, just grabbing a coffee."

Her smile broadened, revealing perfectly white teeth. "Well, in that case, how about I buy you a coffee as a way of saying sorry for bumping into you?"

Though David's initial instinct was to decline politely, the prospect of a free coffee, especially given his wallet conundrum, tempted him. A smile crept onto his lips, and he accepted her offer. "Sure, that's very kind of you."

She gestured towards an empty table by the window. "Shall we sit?"

Setting aside his coffee crisis for the moment, David followed her to the table, taking a seat and wondering where this encounter might lead.

The woman introduced herself as Sara, and the conversation flowed naturally.

Sara started with light small talk, asking about David's day and how he found himself in Knightsbridge. David found himself hesitating to answer her questions, unsure of how much to disclose to a stranger.

Sara noticed his hesitation and leaned in, her blue eyes filled with curiosity. "I hope I'm not prying too much."

David offered a weak smile, attempting to find a balance between honesty and privacy. "No, not at all."

The conversation continued, but it took an unexpected turn when Sara delved into David's personal life. "So, are you seeing anyone? Do you have a boyfriend?"

David was taken aback by the abrupt question. He hadn't disclosed his sexuality or relationship status, and it seemed odd that she would inquire about such personal matters. Deciding not to disclose his sexual orientation or his relationship with Ryan, he replied casually, "No, I'm not seeing anyone at the moment."

Sara's interest in his love life persisted, leading to more probing questions about his preferences and past relationships. With each inquiry, David felt increasingly uneasy. He hadn't anticipated such a personal interrogation during a chance encounter with a stranger.

The conversation eventually circled back to coffee, and Sara insisted on paying for his cup despite his protests. As David thanked her and made his exit from the coffee shop, he couldn't shake the lingering sense of relief mixed with perplexity. Something about the interaction felt off, and he was left with lingering questions about Sara's unusual interest in his personal life.

Determined to put the peculiar encounter behind him, David headed home, eager to address his wallet situation with Ryan.

David had successfully navigated his way back to their flat without any issues, his solo exploration leaving him with a sense of accomplishment. He opened the front door to find Ryan already at home, his hair and body was dripping wet from what seemed like a shower. David tried his best not to openly drool.

"Hey, where have you been?" Ryan inquired as he busily dried his hair.

"I decided to go out and explore today while you were at work. You weren't there long," David replied, walking over to where Ryan stood and giving him a welcoming kiss.

"Yeah, Craig wanted me in since they were short a trainer at the gym today. How did your walk go?" Ryan asked, his curiosity piqued.

David thought for a moment, realising that Ryan had never really mentioned where he worked before. "Huh. You never really mentioned where you worked before. And my walk had been great, though something strange happened."

"Strange? In what way?" Ryan asked, now pulling clothes from his bag.

David recounted the unusual encounter at the coffee shop, and Ryan looked just as puzzled as he had been during the conversation. "Also, did you find out anything about my belongings from the Detective?"

Ryan sighed, his expression shifting to one of concern. "Yeah, sorry, I forgot to tell you that they still have your belongings in the evidence locker. They still don't know how long they'll have them there at the moment. I'll check again for you," he assured David.

"That would be great," David said, squeezing Ryan in a hug as soon as he was dressed.

Ryan then made a suggestion. "Do you want to come with me?"

David looked curious. "Why? Where are we going?"

Ryan explained with a hint of excitement, "Well, since I am moving here, I need to go and get some of my stuff from my old place."

David was genuinely interested. "Will there be a lot to move?"

Ryan reassured him, "No, the furniture was provided by my landlord.

The only things I owned there were my clothes and supplements and some other things."

David considered this and inquired further, "Okay. Do we need a bigger bag?"

Ryan offered a loving smile. "Just a small luggage should be fine since I could always call a moving company for the rest of my stuff. I already took most of my clothes there earlier since work is nearby."

"Okay. I think I saw one somewhere in the house," David said, trying to remember where he had found the luggage.

Ryan, ever attentive, took charge. "Go sit down; I know where it is. You just got home, and you need to relax for a bit."

David nodded and took a seat in the living room, Tyson joining him. While David settled in, Ryan fetched the luggage from its storage spot.

"Ready?" Ryan asked as he reappeared with the luggage in tow.

David nodded, and they headed out together. Ryan called for a cab, a practical choice given they were going to retrieve Ryan's belongings from his previous place. Their day was filled with errands and shared moments, reinforcing the sense of togetherness that was quickly becoming their new normal.

25

David

NAVIGATING THROUGH THE ENDURING TRAFFIC OF LONDON, was an experience akin to a rite of passage, extended their cab ride considerably.

David, his curiosity piqued by the ever-changing cityscape, leaned closer to Ryan amid the hum of vehicles.

"So, Ryan, is this where you live? Looks a bit... shadier than I expected," David remarked, his gaze drifting to the neighbourhood

Ryan chuckled, his arm casually wrapped around David. "Ah, this place. We used to call it Shady Street."

Raised eyebrows and intrigue followed. "Shady Street? Why's that?"

A grin tugged at Ryan's lips as he began to unravel the tale. "Well, it's not the fanciest neighbourhood, as you can see. But it's home."

David nodded, his understanding laced with respect. The journey to self-sufficiency often started with modest surroundings. "I respect that, Ryan. It's your space, and that's what matters."

The cab eventually deposited them in front of a nondescript building in Hackney, and David couldn't help but wonder what lay beyond the door of Ryan's flat. After paying the fare, they made their way up a flight of stairs to Ryan's flat. What awaited inside was a stark contrast to the exterior.

Ryan's flat boasted impeccable cleanliness, efficient organization, and modern furnishings that exuded a cozy ambiance. The stark transformation from the external environment left David genuinely impressed.

"Wow, Ryan, your place is… really nice," David complimented, taking in the tasteful decor.

Ryan's smile was tinged with pride. "Thanks, David. I've put a lot of effort into making it cozy."

Their tour led them to the living room, where a comfy sofa faced a modest-sized TV, surrounded by potted plants for a touch of greenery. A well-kept bookshelf held a collection of books and cherished keepsakes, lending the room character.

David couldn't help but draw comparisons to his opulent surroundings in Knightsbridge. However, he understood that what truly mattered was the care and love invested in a place.

Curious about Ryan's journey to this cozy haven, David asked, "How did you end up here, Ryan?"

Ryan, taking a moment to reflect on his past, began to share his story. "When I first moved to London, I was just starting out. Money was tight, and this was all I could afford. I've worked hard to make it my own and create a comfortable space for myself. It's not much, but it's home."

David nodded, fully grasping the sentiment. "It's your sanctuary, and it's lovely."

Their focus shifted back to the task at hand, and they began packing some of Ryan's clothes into the luggage they had brought along. Ryan, with meticulous care, folded each garment and arranged them neatly in the suitcase. David joined in, appreciating the simplicity of the task.

Ryan gathered his daily supplements, a testament to his unwavering dedication to his health. It was a routine born of resilience and determination.

With the packing now complete, they settled on the bed, side by side, shoulders brushing against each other. David couldn't help but look around the room once more, a profound appreciation filling him. It was more than just a space; it was a testament to Ryan's journey, hard work, and the creation of a loving and welcoming home.

Their gazes met, and in that shared moment, David leaned in, their lips meeting in a soft, tender kiss, a silent affirmation of their bond.

Breaking the kiss, David whispered, "No matter where we are, as long as we're together, it's home, Ryan."

Ryan's smile radiated warmth. "That's all I ever wanted, David."

They stood up from the bed and David stumbled upon a hidden sport shirt under Ryan's bed. It was a seemingly ordinary garment, bearing the number twelve, but as he held it in his hands, an unexpected wave of sensations washed over him. A strange mix of confusion and déjà vu enveloped his senses, and then, a vivid scene unfurled in David's mind.

It was a rare sunny day in London, and the atmosphere was filled with the buzz of friends gathered for a sports day in the park. David stood on the sidelines, watching Ryan in a rugby jersey with the number twelve emblazoned on the back. Ryan's determination was evident as he charged across the field, the game reaching its intense climax. But then, a sudden collision sent Ryan sprawling onto the grass, clutching his injured ankle.

Without hesitation, David rushed to his friend's side. His face was etched with concern as he knelt beside Ryan, drowning out the shouts for help from others. In that moment, David's sole focus was on his injured friend.

"Ryan, you with me?" David whispered softly, his voice filled with worry.

Ryan grimaced but managed a nod. "Yeah, I'm here. It hurts, though."

With gentle care, David examined the injury, his fingers tracing over the swollen ankle. "You're going to be okay, just hold on."

He helped Ryan to his feet, and with the support of their friends, they made their way to a nearby bench. Throughout the hours that followed, David's care and concern never wavered as he tended to his injured friend. Their bond grew stronger during that time, a testament to the unspoken understanding they shared.

The return to the present was abrupt and jarring. David found himself back in Ryan's room, the sport shirt cradled in his hands. His heart raced, and his breaths came in short gasps as he grappled with the unexpected onslaught of memories.

Ryan, sensing David's distress, turned toward him with genuine concern etched across his face. "David, are you okay?"

David took a moment to gather his thoughts, his hands still trembling as they clutched the sport shirt. He managed to find his voice, though it quivered with emotion. "I remember this shirt, Ryan."

Ryan's brows furrowed in confusion, but his eyes remained locked onto David's, searching for answers.

"It's from that rugby game, the sports day," David continued, his voice now filled with heartfelt nostalgia.

Recognition dawned in Ryan's eyes as he pieced together the fragments of the memory. He remembered that day, the shared experiences, and the injury that had drawn them closer. It was a moment etched in their history, a testament to the strength of their friendship and, eventually, their love.

Ryan's touch was gentle as he reached out, his hand cupping David's cheek. "You remember, David?"

Tears welled up in David's eyes, but they were tears of remembrance, of a bond that had withstood the tests of time and adversity. "Yes, I remember, Ryan."

Ryan's voice carried a reassuring tone, filled with hope. "We're getting there, David. We're going to fully recover your memories."

Without another word, Ryan pulled David into a warm and comforting hug.

26

Ryan

ONCE AGAIN, RYAN FOUND HIMSELF in the tricky position of leaving David home alone, which he really didn't want to do. But duty called, and this time, he had a little surprise in the works for David.

Ryan had gone out and picked up a temporary phone for David. He knew that David was itching to get back to his normal routine, especially since his phone was still locked away in the evidence locker. The plan was to give it to David when he got home from work, but as usual, things got a bit sidetracked.

Ryan placed the gift box, containing the shiny new temporary phone, on the bedside table. He also added an old Oyster card that had some credit on it and a bit of cash, just in case David got the itch to explore the city. Then, with a gentle kiss on David's forehead and a pat on Tyson's head, he left the room.

It wasn't easy for Ryan to leave David behind after what had happened the night before. But he had an important reason for his absence this time.

As he closed the door behind him, Ryan's heart was heavy with guilt, but there was also a sense of excitement in the air. He had a surprise birthday celebration to plan for David, and that thought kept his spirits high. Each step he took away from their home was filled with thoughts of David's reaction when he discovered the temporary phone and the fantastic birthday bash that was taking shape.

Ryan's first stop was, of course, SugarBliss. He had gotten to know the friendly barista behind the counter over time, and her warm smile greeted him as he entered the bakery.

"Hey there, Ryan! How can I help you today?" she asked with that cheerful tone of hers.

Ryan returned her smile, feeling instantly comforted by the bakery's inviting ambiance. "Are Irene and Lucas around? I was hoping to catch them."

The barista gave a knowing nod. "They're in the kitchen. Shall I give them a heads-up?"

Ryan decided to go for the element of surprise. "Nah, I'll just pop in. Thanks!"

With a friendly wave to the barista, he made his way towards the kitchen where David's parents were busy at work. The moment he stepped inside, Irene and Lucas looked up, their faces breaking into surprised smiles.

"Well, look who's here!" Irene greeted, her eyes lighting up with genuine pleasure.

Ryan returned their warm welcome, settling into the familiar atmosphere. "Hey Irene and Lucas, do you have a minute?"

Lucas, his hands still coated with flour, wiped them on his apron and joined Irene in putting their work on hold. "Of course, Ryan. What's on your mind?"

Ryan leaned in, eager to share his plans. "I've got a little surprise in mind for David's birthday."

David's parents leaned in, their curiosity piqued. Irene placed the customer's order aside, and they both focused on Ryan, their eyes filled with anticipation.

As Ryan began to lay out his ideas for the surprise party, Irene and Lucas listened intently. They exchanged quick glances and nodded in agreement. Ryan couldn't help but notice a playful glint in their eyes.

"Is there something you two aren't telling me?" he asked with a grin, sensing there was more to their reactions.

Irene chuckled warmly, sharing a knowing look with her husband. "You caught us, Ryan. We've been brewing up a little surprise of our own for David's birthday."

Lucas chimed in, "And we've got some of his favourite cookies in the works for the party."

Ryan laughed, relieved that their secret was nothing but a delightful surprise. "Well, it looks like we're all in sync here."

The three of them continued discussing party details and sharing stories about their experiences with David. Laughter filled the air as they brainstormed ideas, and Ryan couldn't help but feel immense gratitude for the close bond he shared with Irene and Lucas.

Before he left, Irene handed Ryan a container filled with freshly baked cookies. "Here you go, Ryan. A little sneak peek of what we've got in store for the party."

Ryan accepted the sweet gift with a grateful smile. "Thanks a bunch."

Once they said their goodbyes, Ryan left their bakery and headed to his next stop, which was in Embankment. As he strolled towards the tube station, his phone started ringing. Glancing at the caller ID, he saw that it was David calling, bringing an immediate grin to his face. Ryan had set up David's new phone with his number so they could stay connected easily.

"Hey there, sweetheart," Ryan greeted, hearing the familiar sound of David stretching. "Just woke up, huh?"

"I did, and you're nowhere to be found again. Should I start keeping you tied up in bed, mister?" David teased, playfully hinting at their more intimate moments, which always sent a shiver of desire down Ryan's spine.

"Well, if you're volunteering, maybe I should consider leaving you in bed more often," Ryan retorted, his voice taking on a seductive undertone.

"Don't you dare! I miss you already," David replied with a hint of longing in his voice.

"I know, babe, but I won't be gone for long. Got a few things to sort out, and then I'll be back in no time," Ryan reassured him.

"Speaking of things, did you really get me a phone? You didn't have to do that," David said, his tone filled with gratitude.

"Yeah, well, thought it might come in handy while your old one's stuck in evidence locker. So, any plans for the day?" Ryan inquired, eager to hear what David had in mind.

David pondered for a moment before responding, "I don't have any concrete plans, but I was thinking about going to the park today and taking Tyson for a walk. Do we have a leash for him?"

"David, that cat barely moves around inside the house, and you want to take him to a park," Ryan chuckled.

"It's worth a shot. So, do we have a leash?" David inquired once more.

"No, we don't have a leash for him. You got him a stroller a while back, and I think it's hidden next to his food bowl," Ryan replied.

"Ugh, moving. I'll have to look for it later," David groaned, and Ryan couldn't help but chuckle at his reaction.

"Alright, just promise me that if anything feels off, you'll give me a call," Ryan said, knowing he had to trust David's judgment.

"I promise. Now go run your errands so we can have some fun tonight," David teased, his playful tone sparking Ryan's desire. Ryan was full-on Stonehenge at this point and was trying hard to hide it.

"Stop it, you're going to turn me into a public menace," Ryan chuckled, thoroughly enjoying their banter.

David laughed on the other end. "See you later, babe."

"Take care!" Ryan replied before ending the call.

Ryan stepped off the tube at Embankment station, twenty minutes later than planned. He had arranged to meet Layla, who was working at a bar in the area today. As he made his way up the stairs, lost in thought, he inadvertently bumped into someone. Looking up, he was surprised to see Detective Wayne.

"Detective, what brings you here?" Ryan greeted him, offering a handshake.

"Ryan," Detective Wayne replied, returning the handshake. "I was just here because someone gave us a call saying that they may have some information on David's case."

Ryan's heart quickened with anticipation. "Can you tell me what you found out?"

The Detective's expression remained stoic. "Not yet, not until we're certain that this person was telling the truth. For now, all I can tell you is that we've got a good lead if this person's statement can be verified."

Ryan understood the need for caution. "I appreciate the update. Any progress on retrieving anything from David's phone and wallet?"

Detective Wayne reached into his coat pocket and pulled out David's wallet. "Actually, I was just headed to the Millers to return David's wallet. As for his phone, we're still working on accessing it. Once we extract all the messages, we'll be able to return it to him."

"Thank you," Ryan said with genuine gratitude. "David's been looking for this."

The Detective nodded and gave Ryan a pat on the back. "I've got to get going, Ryan. Say hi to David for me."

As Detective Wayne walked away, Ryan felt a renewed sense of hope. The pieces of the puzzle were slowly coming together, and he couldn't wait to share the news with David.

Ryan headed over to the bar where Layla was working. The morning sun cast a warm glow over the city as he approached, and Layla's familiar figure came into focus. She was already waving enthusiastically, her bright smile a welcoming sight. The bar, typically closed in the morning, had its doors ajar as the staff prepared for the day ahead.

As Ryan reached Layla, their customary hug was a comfortable reassurance of their friendship. Layla's eyes sparkled with curiosity as she asked about David's well-being. Ryan responded with a reassuring grin, his gratitude evident. "David's doing okay, Layla. Some of his memories are starting to come back."

Layla's excitement was infectious as she pulled Ryan into another heartfelt hug. Breaking the embrace, they stepped back, ready to dive into the nitty-gritty of their planning.

"So, spill the beans, Ryan. Tell me everything about David's surprise birthday bash," Layla urged, her enthusiasm palpable.

Ryan couldn't help but share in her excitement as they began brainstorming ideas and sharing their visions for the celebration. Even in the morning light, the bar's atmosphere was charged with anticipation.

"I was thinking we keep it low-key," Ryan began, his voice brimming with enthusiasm. "Invite a few close friends and family to David's place."

Layla nodded eagerly, her eyes shining with creative ideas. "That sounds perfect, Ryan. We could decorate with photos and memories from David's life."

Ryan's smile grew wider at the thought, touched by Layla's heartfelt suggestion. "Exactly. I want him to feel surrounded by love and familiarity. Oh, and we can't forget Tyson. Maybe a tiny party hat for him?"

Layla burst into laughter, the sound filling the bar. "Oh, Tyson in a party hat would be adorable. Count me in for that."

Their planning flowed seamlessly as they built on each other's ideas. They discussed themes, colours, and how to keep the surprise from David. Layla even proposed a meaningful gift, an idea that resonated deeply with Ryan.

As they continued their discussions, Ryan couldn't help but feel grateful for Layla's unwavering support and camaraderie. She had been a pillar of strength for both him and David during their toughest moments, and this birthday celebration was a testament to their enduring friendship.

Before parting ways to continue their preparations, Layla flashed Ryan a warm smile. "This is going to be amazing, Ryan. David will be so touched by all of this."

Ryan shared her enthusiasm, his heart swelling with anticipation. "I believe so too, Layla. Thanks for being a part of it."

With a final exchange of ideas and a promise to meet again soon, Ryan left the bar with a renewed sense of purpose. The surprise birthday party for David was shaping up beautifully, and he couldn't wait to see the joy it would bring to his partner's heart.

Ryan couldn't wait to get back home. The sun was lazily making its way down, casting a warm, golden glow into their flat in Knightsbridge.

When he stepped through the door, a sense of calm washed over him. It was home, his sanctuary, and David was waiting for him.

David came out of the bedroom with a welcoming smile on his face. His eyes held affection, and his lips curved into a playful grin. There was a silent understanding between them, a connection that transcended the challenges they faced.

Without words, David walked up to Ryan, a sense of purpose in his steps. Their eyes locked, and for a moment, it felt like it was just the two of them. David's fingers lightly traced Ryan's jawline, conveying a longing that words couldn't capture.

Ryan mirrored the gesture, his hands finding their way to David's waist, pulling him close. Their bodies pressed together, the warmth seeping through their clothes, and their hearts beating in unison. The anticipation had been building, a testament to their profound connection.

Their lips met in a hungry, passionate kiss. It was a kiss filled with longing, a silent acknowledgment of the moments they'd missed being apart, and the overpowering need to be close again. Their tongues danced together, an intimate rhythm that promised the intensity to come.

As their lips remained locked, they began to undress each other, hands exploring every familiar curve and contour. Buttons were undone, zippers lowered, and layers of fabric fell to the floor in a sensual strip tease. Their eyes never strayed from each other, their gazes smouldering with desire.

Ryan's hands roamed over David's body, every touch sparking a fire within. He marvelled at the softness of David's skin, the gentle rise and fall of his chest as their breath quickened. David's fingertips brushed over Ryan's flesh, leaving a trail of goosebumps in their wake.

As their bodies melded, they stumbled toward the bedroom, guided by instinct and longing. The sheets, soft and inviting, welcomed them, and they tumbled onto the bed, a tangle of limbs and desire. Their kisses grew deeper, more fervent, as their hands continued their exploration.

Ryan's lips found their way to David's neck, nibbling and teasing. David arched his back, a low moan escaping his lips. The room filled with the symphony of their desire, a harmonious blend of gasps, whispers, and the rapid rhythm of their heartbeats.

"Ryan," David gasped, his voice filled with need. "I've missed you."

"I've missed you too, David," Ryan murmured between kisses, his voice husky with desire.

Their movements became more urgent, fuelled by their shared

longing. The room was filled with the intoxicating scent of their passion, a fragrance that hung in the air as they held each other close. Their breaths gradually slowed, and their hearts beat in harmony, a testament to the deep connection they shared.

In the afterglow of their passionate union, they lay together, limbs entwined, their fingers tracing lazy patterns on each other's skin. Words were unnecessary; their love spoke through their actions, through the tenderness of their touch.

As they drifted into a contented slumber, wrapped in each other's arms, they knew that no matter what challenges lay ahead.

27

David

"THE HOSPITAL CALLED. They want us to come back to see if they can get your stitches out," Ryan informed, getting up, but his teasing tone didn't fade. "Don't worry, we've got enough time for breakfast. I know how you are in the mornings." David playfully threw a pillow at Ryan, their laughter a testament to their easygoing morning banter. "Oh, and Detective Wayne finally returned your wallet yesterday when I bumped into him."

Inspecting the wallet, David found it intact, cash included. He looked back at Ryan with a playful glint. "Looks like I have some cash left. How about I treat you to breakfast?"

Ryan's attention shifted entirely to David. "Sounds good. A Starbucks run it is."

With breakfast plans in mind, David got out of bed, ready to seize the day with Ryan by his side. "Let's roll. Time to get ready," he suggested, sealing the morning with another affectionate kiss before heading to shower.

David basked in the warmth of the shower, steam swirling around him, and his senses heightened as he sensed Ryan's presence drawing near. The shower door slid open, and there he was, Ryan, with that mischievous glint in his eye, a silent invitation David couldn't resist.

Ryan didn't waste a second. He stepped into the shower, and their eyes locked, sparking an unspoken understanding. No words were needed; the promise of desire hung heavy in the air.

Ryan's wet fingers traced tantalising patterns on David's slick skin, making him shiver with anticipation. Water droplets danced down their bodies as if in celebration of their union.

Without a word, their mouths met in a fiery kiss. It was a dance of passion, lips and tongues moving with an unspoken rhythm. David's breath hitched, and he felt intoxicated by the connection they shared.

Ryan's hands were a revelation, teasing and possessive as they explored every inch of David's body. It was as if each touch conveyed a deeper message of their profound connection, igniting an irresistible fire within.

"Ryan…" David moaned

"What do you want baby?"

"You… Please…" David's body felt like it was on overdrive and had no control over it.

"So needy." Ryan chuckled and continued touching David's already too hot body.

But David wasn't to be outdone. His own hands mirrored Ryan's ardor, seeking to explore every nuance of Ryan's sculpted form. Wet strands of hair tangled between their fingers, and their lips left trails of heat on wet skin. Soft sighs filled the steamy air, a sensual symphony of desire.

As the shower continued to rain down on them, Ryan gently guided David backward until they stood together beneath the cascading water. It intensified their connection, their bodies pressed against each other, yearning for more of the electrifying contact that set them ablaze.

Their unspoken communication led to a graceful exchange of roles, and now it was David's turn to pay homage to Ryan's body. Wet kisses traced a fiery path along Ryan's jaw, down to his neck, and further south to explore the contours of his chest. The rhythm of Ryan's heartbeat became a hypnotic melody that fuelled their passion.

Their bodies moved in unison, generating exquisite friction that sent pleasurable shivers coursing through them. David's need for Ryan was undeniable, and he arched into him, craving the electrifying touch that left them both breathless.

They moved with an uncanny synergy, their desires expressed through every touch, kiss, and intimate moan. The steam-filled room became their private haven of sensuality, the outside world dissolving into oblivion as they surrendered to their fervent desires.

"Ryan… Fuck me now… Please…" David moaned

"Yeah? You want my cock inside you?"

"If you don't fuck me now, I am going to do it myself." David manage to get out.

Ryan's hands explored lower, tracing David's hips, the strength of his thighs, and gripping his buttocks with possessive longing. David's breath hitched, and his fingers dug into Ryan's shoulders as he trembled with anticipation.

Their lovemaking continued, a harmonious blend of passion and connection. The warm water heightened their sensations as they moved together, their hearts pounding in sync, their desires spoken in the language of their bodies.

As they neared the peak of pleasure, their bodies trembled in unison, and they clung to each other, riding waves of ecstasy

In the tender aftermath of their fiery encounter, they remained in each other's arms beneath the cascading water, their bodies inter-twined, their breathing gradually returning to normal.

With a gentle kiss, David whispered, "You mean the world to me."

Ryan held him close, and in that silent embrace, they reaffirmed their love and desire, sealed in the warmth of the steamy shower.

An hour later, they finally got out of their house and fed Tyson, too. Ryan took him to a Starbucks in Oxford Circus and David was surprised too see that it was incredibly busy this early in the morning.

Inside the bustling Starbucks, David and Ryan found themselves in the familiar queue, patiently waiting to place their breakfast orders. Soft chatter and the aromatic promise of coffee filled the air.

As they inched closer to the counter, David couldn't help but overhear Ryan's remark. "You know, this is the same Starbucks we went to on the morning of your attack."

David's curiosity piqued, and he turned to Ryan with a warm smile. "Really? What did we do that day?"

Ryan leaned in, his voice carrying a hint of nostalgia. "We were getting lattes. I remember asking you about the guy you were going to see that night." His gaze softened. "Then we hit up Westfield to buy you some clothes."

David nodded thoughtfully. "Sounds like we had a good time that day."

"We definitely did," Ryan smiled at him.

Their turn in line arrived, and David shifted his attention back to the present. "So, what do I usually order here?" he asked Ryan, intrigued by the prospect of discovering his past preferences.

Ryan's eyes crinkled with amusement as he revealed David's Starbucks staple. "You're a fan of the Pumpkin Spice Latte."

David chuckled. "Pumpkin Spice Latte it is, then." They placed their order for lattes and added some sandwiches to their tray before finding a cozy table by the window.

As they settled into their seats, David's gaze wandered beyond the glass, lost in thought. "What do you think will happen if I ever get all my memories back?"

"It's hard to say for sure. Your memories are a part of who you are, but they don't define you entirely. We've built something beautiful together, and even if your past comes rushing back, I hope it won't change what we have now."

"I agree. Whatever comes, we'll face it together, just like we always have."

Their fingers brushed against each other on the tabletop, a silent reassurance that their bond was unbreakable, even in the face of forgotten memories.

After a satisfying breakfast at Starbucks, David and Ryan decided to head straight to the hospital. David had been looking forward to this appointment because he was more than ready to get the stitches in his head removed. They had become itchy and bothersome, a constant reminder of the incident that had left his memory in tatters. While David knew he would carry a scar on his shaved head for the rest of his life, it didn't bother him as much as it once had. In fact, he had grown somewhat fond of his new look.

As they walked toward the hospital,David couldn't help but rub his smooth scalp and offer a contented smile. "You know, I never thought I'd say this, but I'm actually starting to like the bald look."

Ryan glanced at him, his eyes filled with genuine affection. "David, you look amazing no matter what. And if you're worried about it, your hair should grow back soon."

David's heart fluttered at Ryan's sweet words. With their fingers intertwined, they made their way to Dr. Christiansen's office, the same doctor who had been monitoring David's progress since the incident. The doctor greeted them with a warm smile, motioning for them to take a seat.

"How are you both doing?" Dr. Christiansen inquired, his concern evident.

David glanced at Ryan before answering. "We're getting there. Some of my memories are starting to come back."

The doctor nodded, pleased with the news. "And how about the headaches? Are they still bothering you?"

David shook his head. "No, actually. I haven't had a headache in a while now."

Dr. Christiansen smiled reassuringly. "That's great to hear, David. It seems like your recovery is progressing well."

With that, the doctor proceeded to examine David's stitches, gently removing the sutures with skilful hands. David focused on his breathing, feeling a sense of relief as each stitch came out. Ryan watched the procedure with a supportive smile, his presence providing comfort.

Finally, the doctor declared, "All done. The stitches are out, but be sure to be careful with the area for a while. It's healing nicely."

David nodded, feeling lighter now that the stitches were gone. He glanced at Ryan, who was positively beaming with pride. They knew this was a small but significant step toward normalcy.

Before leaving the doctor's office, Dr. Christiansen offered some parting words of encouragement. "Remember, if you ever need anything or have any concerns, don't hesitate to reach out. We're here to support you both."

With their appointment successfully completed, David and Ryan made their way out of the hospital.

Once they stepped outside the hospital, David felt a sense of relief and newfound energy. He turned to Ryan with a hopeful smile and a glint of excitement in his eyes.

"You know, Ryan, I was thinking," David began, "since we've just had my stitches removed and everything's going well, how about we go and recreate that morning we had on the day of my attack?"

Ryan's brows furrowed with concern as he considered David's suggestion. He didn't want David to push himself too hard, especially after what he had been through. "Are you sure that's a wise idea, babe? I don't want you to overexert yourself."

David chuckled and gently placed a hand on Ryan's cheek, his thumb caressing his skin. "Ryan, I promise I'll be fine. Besides, I really want to do this."

Ryan couldn't resist the sincerity in David's gaze. He leaned in and placed a tender kiss on David's lips, a silent reassurance that he would support his decision. "Alright, if you're sure, let's do it."

With their plan set, they headed to Westfield in Shepherd's Bush, a massive shopping centre that was bustling with activity.

As they entered the shopping centre, David couldn't help but let his jaw drop at the sheer size and grandeur of the place. It was a shopper's paradise, a haven for retail therapy, and it was easy to see why it had been one of David's favourite places to shop and unwind.

Ryan chuckled at David's awestruck expression. "Impressive, isn't it? You used to drag me all over this place, telling me stories about each store we passed."

David grinned as memories of their past outings flooded back. "I can see why. This place is amazing."

They strolled through the shopping centre, their hands intertwined. David took in the sights and sounds, occasionally stopping at stores to explore and reminisce. Ryan played along, sharing stories and anecdotes about their previous visits.

Eventually, they found themselves in the food court, where a variety of delicious aromas filled the air. David's stomach couldn't help but growl at the tempting scents. They decided to grab some yogurt from a nearby vendor and settled at a table.

As they enjoyed their yogurt, Ryan turned his attention to David. "So, how are you feeling, David?"

David took a moment to reflect on the day and their journey. His eyes softened as he looked at Ryan. "Honestly, Ryan, I've never felt better. And it's all thanks to you."

Ryan's heart swelled with affection, and he reached across the table to gently cup David's cheek. "You don't know how happy that makes me, David."

As David and Ryan sat in the bustling food court, enjoying their yogurt and each other's company, David's attention was drawn to a familiar figure out of the corner of his eyes. He turned to look, but the person seemed to have vanished into the crowd. A puzzled expression crossed David's face, and Ryan immediately picked up on his unease.

"Hey, what's wrong?" Ryan asked, concern etching his features.

David hesitated for a moment, trying to make sense of what he had just glimpsed. "I thought I saw someone I knew, but they disappeared. Must have been my imagination."

Ryan's worry eased slightly, but he kept a watchful eye on David. "Are you sure you're okay?"

David nodded, though a lingering sense of unease remained. "Yeah, I'm fine. It's probably just my mind playing tricks on me."

Ryan leaned in closer, his voice soft and reassuring. "If you ever feel uncomfortable or need to leave, just let me know, alright?"

David offered a grateful smile, touched by Ryan's consideration. "Thanks, Ryan. I appreciate it."

They continued to enjoy their yogurt, but the strange encounter had left a shadow over David's mood. He finally decided to change the subject, wanting to focus on something positive. Turning to Ryan, he asked, "Do you mind if we stop by the Tesco near our house after this?"

Ryan raised an eyebrow, curious about David's request. "Of course, but may I ask why?"

David's eyes sparkled with enthusiasm as he explained, "I've been practicing my cooking skills while you were at work, and I thought it would be nice if, for a change, I cooked dinner for you tonight. So, I need to grab some ingredients."

A warm smile spread across Ryan's face as he listened to David's idea. "That sounds amazing, David. I'd love to taste your cooking. What's on the menu?"

David leaned in closer, excitement bubbling in his voice. "Well, I was thinking of making that spaghetti carbonara recipe that the recipe book said you love so much."

Ryan chuckled with delight. "You've been busy, haven't you? Spaghetti carbonara sounds perfect. Let's head to Tesco after this, and you can grab everything you need."

With their plans set and the promise of a delicious meal ahead, David's earlier unease began to fade. He was eager to continue exploring new experiences and making lasting memories with Ryan, one meal at a time.

28

David

A FEW DAYS HAD PASSED since David got his stitches removed and David found himself sitting at the kitchen table, sipping a cup of tea, and enjoying the comforting familiarity of his parents' house. Ryan had dropped him off earlier, promising to return later in the day, and David couldn't help but feel a sense of contentment.

David noticed his Mum, bustling about the room. She moved with a grace born of years of practice, effortlessly preparing breakfast for the two of them.

David's Mum turned to him with a warm smile, her eyes crinkling at the corners as she set a plate of freshly cooked pancakes in front of him. "There you go, love. Pancakes, just the way you like them."

"Thanks, Mum," David replied, returning her smile.

He appreciated his Mum's efforts to make him feel at home.

"So, David, how are you and Ryan doing? Your father and I are so glad to hear that he's moved in with you."

"We're doing really well, Mum," he replied, his voice filled with warmth. "Having Ryan with me has been amazing. He's been so supportive, especially with everything that's happened."

His Mum nodded, her expression filled with understanding. "I can imagine how important that support must be, especially after what you've been through." She paused, her gaze gentle. "You know, David, we've always known that you and Ryan had something special. It warms my heart to see you two together."

David couldn't help but smile. "I'm really lucky to have him, Mum."

His Mum reached across the table, placing a hand on David's. Her touch was comforting, a silent affirmation of their bond. "And he's lucky to have you too, dear."

Their conversation continued as they enjoyed their breakfast, the familiar banter and laughter filling the kitchen. David felt a deep sense of gratitude for these moments, for the love and warmth that enveloped him in his parents' home.

The two of them cleared the table together, washing the dishes in companionable silence.

Ryan had been by his side through it all, a steadfast presence in his life. David knew that Ryan had been acting a little strangely in the past couple of days, but he had decided not to question him about it.

He trusted that Ryan would share what was on his mind when he was ready.

David's thoughts returned to Ryan's decision to move in with him. David was both excited and grateful for the opportunity to build a life together. He knew that there would be challenges along the way, but he was confident that they could face anything as long as they were together.

Once the kitchen was tidy, David and his Mum settled into the living room, chatting about everything and nothing. It was a perfect morning, filled with the kind of warmth and love that only family could provide.

As David sipped his tea, he felt a sense of contentment wash over him. He had come a long way since that fateful night when.

After a while, David found himself sitting on the edge of his childhood bed, surrounded by the familiar sights and sounds of his parents' home. It was close to lunchtime, and the memories of his teenage years flooded back as he gazed around the room. His Mum had suggested that spending time in his old room might trigger some forgotten memories, but David was skeptical. Still, he appreciated her efforts to help him recover his lost past.

David absentmindedly ran his fingers over the fabric of the covers, the texture of the familiar bed linens grounding him in the present. His mind wandered, and he couldn't help but reflect on the twists and turns of his life, especially his relationship with Ryan.

David couldn't help but wonder about the path not taken. What if he had acted on his feelings for Ryan when they were teenagers? Would their relationship be different now? Would they still be as close and in love as they were? These were questions that occasionally crept into his thoughts, but David knew deep down that every decision he had made had brought him to where he was today—with Ryan by his side, unwavering in his support and love.

David's hand idly swept across the bed, and he felt something unusual beneath his pillow. Curiosity piqued, he retrieved the hidden object—a letter. It was dated just three days before the attack, a time when he still had all his memories intact. His hands trembled as he carefully unfolded the paper, revealing the words he had penned to Ryan. The contents of the letter flooded his vision, and David began to read.

Dear Ryan,

I've been doing a lot of thinking lately, and there's something I need to share with you. These feelings have been building up inside me for a while now, and I can't keep them to myself any longer. It's both a confession and a promise, so please bear with me as I try to put my thoughts into words.

I want you to know that I love you, Ryan. More than just a friend, more than anyone else in my life. It's a kind of love that's deep and profound, the kind that transcends words. I can't pinpoint exactly when it happened, but somewhere along the way, you became my everything.

But, here's the thing—I don't want my feelings to hold you back or make you feel burdened. You deserve the world, and I won't stand in your way if you ever find someone who can give you that. I'll step aside if that's what's best for you, even if it breaks my heart.

No matter what happens, Ryan, please know that my love for you will endure. It won't change, no matter where life takes us. Even if we're just friends or if you find love elsewhere, my feelings for you are unwavering. I'll always be here for you, cheering you on from the sidelines, supporting your dreams, and celebrating your happiness.

So, whatever path you choose, please do it with all your heart. Pursue your dreams, find love, and never settle for anything less than what makes you truly happy. If that happiness leads you away from me, I'll understand. Just promise me one thing—that you'll always remember the bond we share, the moments we've cherished, and the love that has defined a significant part of my life.

Take care of yourself, Ryan. You deserve all the happiness in the world.

With all my love,

David

As David read the words he had penned all those days ago, his heart swelled with a mix of emotions. The letter was a bittersweet reminder of his deep feelings for Ryan, feelings that had endured even through the darkest of times.

Tears welled up in David's eyes, a mixture of nostalgia and gratitude. He realised that, despite the uncertainties of their past and present, he had never truly let go of Ryan in his heart. Their bond was unbreakable, a testament to the strength of their connection.

David clutched the letter in his hand, lost in a whirlwind of emotions as he sat on the edge of his childhood bed. He hadn't realised that he was still gripping the letter when he heard a gentle knock on the door.

The door slowly swung open, and there, standing in the doorway, was Ryan. His presence brought an immediate sense of comfort and reassurance to David.

Ryan's warm eyes met David's, filled with concern. Without a word, he moved closer and sat down beside David, who was still in a daze.

David felt the gentle touch of Ryan's fingers as he cupped David's face, wiping away the tears that had escaped during his emotional moment.

"What's wrong?" Ryan asked softly, his voice filled with genuine worry.

David hesitated for a moment, his thoughts scattered. He finally spoke, his words heavy with the hypothetical scenario that had weighed on his mind. "Ryan, what would you have done if I'd decided to let you go?"

Ryan's brows furrowed in confusion. "Let me go? David, what are you talking about?"

David realised that he was still holding the letter and extended it toward Ryan. "Here, read this. It might help you understand."

Ryan took the letter from David's trembling hand and began to read the heartfelt words penned by his partner. As he read, his expression shifted from confusion to contemplation. When he finished, he turned to David, his eyes filled with a mixture of emotions.

David watched Ryan's reaction anxiously, waiting for his response.

Ryan turned to him, and a faint smile tugged at the corners of his lips. "You know, David, I'm really glad you never sent this letter."

David let out a breath he hadn't realised he was holding. He chuckled through his remaining tears. "Yeah, things might have been very different if I had."

Ryan's smile grew warmer as he teased, "Well, we wouldn't want that, would we? I'm not sure I'd be able to resist your cooking if we weren't together."

David couldn't help but laugh, his heart lighter now that he had shared this intimate part of his past with Ryan. He set the letter aside and turned to face him. "You're right. We've come a long way, and I wouldn't change a thing."

Ryan nodded in agreement. "Me neither."

David's heart swelled with affection for the man beside him. "Now, how about we head back home?"

Ryan smiled and stood up, offering his hand to David. "Sounds like a plan. Let's go."

They left the room together, their hands intertwined, and made their way downstairs. David greeted his Mum with a grateful smile and a hug, thanking her for her support. As they prepared to leave, he couldn't help but feel a deep sense of contentment and peace.

As they stepped inside their building, David was taken aback when Ryan asked him to close his eyes. His curiosity piqued, David complied, his heart racing with anticipation. He heard the familiar creak of the door as Ryan opened it, and he followed, guided by Ryan's gentle touch and instructions.

With every step, David's imagination ran wild. What could Ryan be planning? He couldn't help but feel a rush of excitement and curiosity, his trust in Ryan making it easy for him to go along with the surprise. David came to a stop, sensing that they were now inside the threshold of their house.

"Okay, you can open your eyes now," Ryan said with a hint of excitement in his voice.

David's eyes fluttered open, and his breath caught in his throat as he took in the scene before him. The living room was transformed into a festive space filled with familiar faces. Nic, Layla, his Dad, and more friends and loved ones than David could have ever expected. They all shouted in unison, "Surprise! Happy Birthday, David!"

David was overwhelmed with emotion, his eyes misting with tears of joy. He looked around at the beaming faces, feeling a warmth and love that filled the room. His gaze fell on Tyson, wearing a birthday hat, and he couldn't help but chuckle through his tears.

Turning to Ryan, David playfully smacked him on the shoulder. "You sneaky man! You didn't tell me it was my birthday!" Despite the surprise, his heart was brimming with happiness.

Ryan grinned, looking pleased with the success of the surprise. "I had to keep it a secret to make sure it was a real surprise."

David turned to face their guests, his heart swelling with gratitude. "Thank you, everyone. This is incredible." His voice wavered with emotion.

His Dad stepped forward, patting him on the back. "We couldn't let your birthday go unnoticed, son. Now, let's cut the cake!"

David's heart swelled with love as he looked around at the people who cared about him. He couldn't believe how fortunate he was to have them in his life. He had missed out on so much during his amnesia, but moments like this made him realise how much he still had.

Just as they were about to start the festivities, David asked about his Mum. His Dad, with a twinkle in his eye, reassured him, "Don't worry, she'll be here soon."

True to his Dad's words, David's Mum entered the house a short while later, a smile on her face as she joined the celebration. The party was in full swing, with laughter, music, and the clinking of glasses filling the air. David couldn't have asked for a better way to celebrate his birthday. With Ryan by his side and surrounded by their loved ones, he felt truly blessed.

As they gathered around the birthday cake, David made a silent wish, thanking the universe for bringing Ryan back into his life and for the chance to create new memories with the people he loved. It was a day he would never forget, a day that marked the beginning of a new chapter filled with love, laughter, and the promise of a brighter future.

The evening had settled into a cozy, quiet moment after the lively birthday celebration. David found himself snuggled up next to Ryan on the living room couch, feeling content and happy. They basked in the warmth of their shared love, the remnants of joy from the party still lingering in the air.

David shifted slightly, breaking the comfortable silence. "You know what I could really go for right now? Some ice cream."

Ryan turned his head to meet David's gaze, a mischievous smile playing on his lips. "Ice cream, huh? I can make that happen. What flavour are you in the mood for?"

David's eyes lit up as he considered his options. "Surprise me."

Ryan chuckled and planted a quick kiss on David's forehead. "I'll be back in a jiffy."

With that, Ryan got up from the couch and headed towards the front door. He grabbed his jacket and keys, fully intent on making a quick trip to the nearby Tesco to fulfill David's ice cream craving.

David watched him with a fond smile, grateful for the thoughtful gestures that Ryan never ceased to surprise him with.

As the door closed behind Ryan, leaving David and Tyson at home, the quietude of the living room enveloped David. He sank deeper into the couch, enjoying the solitude for a moment.

However, not long after Ryan's departure, David's tranquil evening took an unexpected turn. The doorbell rang, startling him. He wondered why Ryan was back so soon, as he hadn't been gone for long. Puzzled, David made his way to the door and hesitated before opening it.

To his shock and confusion, it wasn't Ryan standing on the doorstep but Sara, from the coffee shop. David's heart raced as he tried to make sense of the situation. He hadn't expected to see her here, especially at his home. His mind raced with questions, but before he could voice any of them, everything spiralled out of control.

Sara moved with startling swiftness, seizing David in a chokehold before he could react. Panic surged through him as he struggled to free himself from her grip, his breaths coming in short gasps. David's mind raced as he grappled with the terrifying realisation that he was being attacked in his own home.

David's thoughts turned to Ryan. He knew that he needed to get out of this dangerous situation and find a way to protect himself. But he couldn't help but wish that Ryan were there with him.

As Sara's hold tightened, David's vision blurred, and his consciousness began to waver. But in the midst of the fear and confusion, he held onto the hope that Ryan would return soon.

29

Ryan

THE EVENING HAD BEEN A BLAST. Ryan couldn't stop smiling as he reminisced about the joy on David's face during the surprise birthday party he'd thrown for him. As he stood in the checkout line at Tesco, clutching David's favorite ice cream, a warm sense of contentment washed over him. Life with David was full of these unexpected delights, and Ryan cherished every one of them.

With a grin on his face, Ryan paid for the ice cream and headed back home to their cozy flat, eager to share the sweet treat with David. Little did he know that the night was about to take an abrupt and terrifying turn.

Approaching their flat, something immediately felt off – the front door was ajar. An ominous knot twisted in Ryan's stomach. Instinct took over as he rushed forward, dropping the ice cream without a second thought. Panic surged within him, and he pushed the door open.

What Ryan found inside their flat was a nightmare come to life. A woman had David trapped in a chokehold, her grip tight and unyielding. Without a moment's hesitation, Ryan lunged forward, his determination propelling him into action. He tore David from the woman's grasp, his heart racing with fear and anger.

The woman, her face now exposed, locked fiery eyes with Ryan. Her blonde wig tumbled to the floor, revealing her true identity – Elle, Ryan's ex-girlfriend. Ryan was stunned, but there was no time to dwell on it. Elle seethed with anger, her voice dripping venom as she spat out her horrifying motives.

"I promised," Elle hissed, her voice trembling with anger. "I promised that whoever took you from me would pay. And now, it's time for you to pay."

Ryan's mind raced as he grappled with the gravity of the situation. Elle held a knife, and her intent was as clear as day. Panic surged through him as he tried to reason with her, to comprehend why she had resorted to such violence. But Elle was beyond reason.

In the frantic seconds that followed, their movements were a blur of desperation and terror. Ryan's mind screamed at him to protect David, to keep him safe from the unpredictable fury of his ex-girlfriend Elle.

As Elle lunged forward with the knife, Ryan's instincts kicked in. He sidestepped her attack, the blade barely grazing his side. The shock of pain shot through him like lightning, but he couldn't let it slow him down. David's life depended on it.

"Ryan, be careful!" David's voice was a mix of fear and urgency.

Ryan grunted as he collided with Elle. Their bodies pressed together, their breaths coming in ragged gasps. The knife clattered to the floor, and Ryan's fingers tightened around Elle's wrist, desperately trying to keep her at bay.

"Why are you doing this, Elle?" Ryan's voice was strained with both anger and disbelief. "We're over. You need to let go."

Elle's face contorted with a mixture of rage and anguish. "You left me, Ryan. You were everything to me, and you just left."

Ryan could see the pain in her eyes, the brokenness that had driven her to this madness. He knew he couldn't reason with her, not in this moment. But he had to protect David.

With a surge of strength, Ryan twisted Elle's wrist, forcing her to release her grip on him. He pushed her away, and she stumbled backward, unsteady on her feet.

David, wide-eyed and trembling, grabbed a nearby lamp. "Stay back, Elle! We don't want to hurt you."

But Elle was beyond reason. With a guttural cry, she lunged for the fallen knife. Ryan couldn't let her reach it. Ignoring the searing pain in his side, he dove towards her, tackling her to the ground.

Their struggle continued on the floor, limbs thrashing and bodies straining. David hovered nearby, torn between fear for Ryan and a deep concern for Elle, a woman he once knew.

"Ryan, please, stop!" David's voice wavered as he called out to his partner. He knew that Ryan was fighting not only for their lives but also for Elle's future.

But Ryan couldn't stop. Not when he had come this far to protect the love of his life. His grip tightened around Elle's wrists, preventing her from reaching the knife. Every moment felt like an eternity as they grappled in the dimly lit room.

Elle's anger had turned into desperation. Tears streamed down her face as she gasped for breath. "You were supposed to love me forever, Ryan. You promised!"

Ryan's heart ached at the pain in her voice, the remnants of a love that had soured into obsession. "I did love you, Elle. But it's over now. You have to let go."

With one final surge of strength, Ryan managed to pin Elle down, her wrists held firmly to the ground. The knife lay just out of her reach. He glanced over at David, his eyes filled with a mixture of relief and worry.

The room was filled with heavy silence, broken only by their labored breathing. Elle's tears continued to fall, her anger dissipating into resignation.

David, ever compassionate, approached slowly. "Elle, we'll get you help. This isn't the way."

Elle nodded weakly, her grip on the knife loosening. The fight had gone out of her, replaced by a profound sadness.

As the police arrived, they found Ryan and David, still holding Elle down. The officers quickly apprehended her and took control of the situation. Ryan's side throbbed with pain, and David rushed to his side, his eyes filled with worry and love.

"Ryan?" David's voice trembled as he gently touched the wound on Ryan's side.

"I love you, David," Ryan whispered, his voice heavy with emotion. "No matter what."

And with those words, his world dissolved into darkness.

30

David

"I LOVE YOU, DAVID. NO MATTER WHAT."

In that crucial moment when Ryan uttered those heartfelt words, David felt like a locked door had been swung open, and a flood of memories came rushing back, crashing into his mind like a torrential downpour. He remembered the night of the attack with chilling clarity—the dark alley, the attackers, the sheer terror that had gripped him. But he also recalled the determination to survive, to fight for his life, and to protect the love he held for Ryan.

Tears welled up in David's eyes as he absorbed these memories, a mix of pain and cherished moments. His job, friends, the cozy coffee shop, and all the moments he had shared with Ryan flooded his mind, both before and after the attack. It was an overwhelming whirlwind of emotions and experiences that threatened to engulf him.

But David couldn't linger in the past, no matter how enticing it was to rediscover his life. His immediate focus shifted back to the present—Ryan, the man he loved, was fighting for his life right before his eyes. Fear and desperation gripped David's heart.

As David glanced at the unconscious Elle on the floor, he knew he had to act swiftly. The knife she had wielded lay nearby, a chilling reminder of the violence she had inflicted. Without hesitation, David kicked the weapon out of her reach, ensuring it couldn't pose any more danger.

The urgency of the situation weighed heavily on him. David reached into Ryan's pocket, his trembling hands fumbling for Ryan's phone. He dialed the emergency number.

The ambulance arrived swiftly, its flashing lights and blaring sirens a beacon of hope amidst the chaos. Paramedics rushed into the flat, their professional training taking over as they assessed Ryan's condition. David could only watch, his heart pounding, as they worked tirelessly to stabilize Ryan and prepare him for transport to the hospital.

Detective Wayne arrived just as the paramedics were preparing to take Ryan to the ambulance. His presence brought a sense of reassurance, a reminder that justice would be pursued.

David's tearful eyes met the detective's, and in that unspoken exchange, they understood each other. There was no need for elaborate words or explanations. The detective had seen the turmoil in David's eyes, the fear and determination that mirrored the intensity of the situation.

Wayne's voice was gentle, conveying both professionalism and empathy. "David, I'll meet you at the hospital to take your statement. Focus on being there for Ryan right now."

David nodded, a mixture of gratitude and concern in his gaze. "Thank you, Detective. Please, make sure Elle faces the consequences of what she's done."

Wayne offered a solemn nod in response. "We'll do everything we can to ensure that, David. You take care of Ryan."

As the ambulance doors closed, David watched it speed away, holding onto the hope that the system would work to hold Elle accountable while he stood by Ryan's side during this critical time.

David held onto Ryan's hand tightly, his heart heavy with worry.

The road ahead was uncertain, but David knew one thing—he would be there for Ryan, unwavering in his love and support, no matter the challenges they faced together.

The hospital's Emergency Room bustled with activity as the EMTs rushed Ryan inside. Panic and urgency filled the air as doctors and nurses mobilized to assess and treat his life-threatening injury. David, standing on the sidelines, felt helpless and overwhelmed.

A kind-hearted nurse, recognizing the fear and anxiety etched across David's face, approached him. She placed a reassuring hand on his shoulder and gently guided him away from the chaotic scene. Her voice was soothing as she said, "Sir, please have a seat in the waiting area. We'll do everything we can for your loved one. We'll keep you informed."

David nodded, his voice barely a whisper. "Thank you."

As he moved to the waiting area, his hands trembling, David realised he needed to notify his parents. His fingers shook as he reached for Ryan's phone, still clutched tightly in Ryan's hand. He dialled the familiar number with urgency, his heart pounding with dread.

"Mum? Dad?" David's voice wavered as he spoke into the phone. "It's David. I need you to come to St. Thomas' Hospital right away. Ryan's been stabbed in the stomach. He's in surgery. Please, hurry."

The concern in his parents' voices was palpable through the phone. They assured David they were on their way and would be at the hospital as quickly as possible.

David hung up and sat in the waiting room, his anxiety mounting with each passing minute. He couldn't shake the fear that had taken hold of his heart. Ryan was everything to him, the love of his life, and the thought of losing him was unbearable.

Time seemed to stretch endlessly as David waited in that sterile, fluorescent-lit room. He stared blankly at the floor, lost in his thoughts, when the entrance to the waiting area suddenly burst open. His parents, with their eyes wide with concern and faces etched with worry, rushed over to where David sat.

Without hesitation, they enveloped him in a tight embrace, their presence offering a modicum of solace in the face of their shared anguish. David held onto them desperately, his tears flowing freely. He needed their support more than ever in this moment of crisis.

"What happened, David?" His Mum's voice was strained, her eyes filled with unshed tears. "Is Ryan going to be okay?"

David's voice quivered as he tried to convey the situation. "Ryan's in surgery right now. Elle got into our flat and started attacking me. Ryan got there in time and fought her but she had a knife on her and stabbed Ryan. The EMTs got there quickly, but… it was bad."

His father's grip tightened on his shoulder, the strength of their familial bond evident. "We're here for you, David. And for Ryan."

David nodded, appreciating his parents' unwavering support. He was grateful that they had arrived so promptly, just when he needed them the most. Together, they waited in the dimly lit waiting room, their collective worry creating an unspoken bond.

As the minutes stretched into hours, David couldn't help but reflect on the tumultuous journey that had brought him to this point. The memories he had recently recovered swirled in his mind, both painful and precious. The love he shared with Ryan had endured every trial and tribulation, and David clung to the hope that it would see them through once more.

Finally, a nurse emerged from the double doors that led to the surgical unit. David's heart leaped into his throat as he stood, his parents beside him, waiting anxiously for any news.

The nurse offered a compassionate smile as she approached. "You're here for Mr. Evans, correct?"

David nodded, his voice barely audible. "Yes, we're here for him."

The nurse proceeded to update them on Ryan's condition. "The surgery went as well as could be expected. The doctors were able to repair the damage and stop the bleeding. Mr. Evans is in the recovery room now, still unconscious. He's stable, but he'll need time to heal."

Relief washed over David, a weight lifting from his shoulders. He turned to his parents, tears of gratitude in his eyes. "He's going to be okay."

His Mum embraced him tightly, tears of relief mingling with his own. "Thank goodness."

The nurse continued to explain the situation. "You can see Mr. Ryan in a little while once he's settled in the recovery room. We'll keep monitoring him closely. He's a fighter, and we'll do everything we can to help him recover."

David thanked the nurse, overwhelmed by her kindness and professionalism. He knew that the battle wasn't over, but at least they had hope on their side.

As they waited for the moment when they could finally see Ryan, David realised that, despite the terrifying ordeal they had just experienced, his memories—both the pain and the joy—had brought him to a profound realisation. His love for Ryan was unwavering and boundless, a force that could overcome even the darkest of trials.

The recovery room provided a moment of respite after the frantic events in the emergency surgery. Soft, gentle lighting bathed the room, and the steady, rhythmic beeping of medical gadgets added a touch of tranquility. David, flanked by his parents, couldn't help but feel a surge of relief and gratitude as they entered.

David made a beeline for Ryan's bedside, where his love lay in a deep slumber. Tubes and machines surrounded Ryan, a testament to the diligent care he was receiving. David took hold of Ryan's hand, feeling the reassuring warmth in his grasp. He leaned in closer, his voice filled with emotion. "Ryan, it's time to wake up. I've got my memory back, and I need you here with me."

Ryan remained serene and still, as if enjoying an afternoon nap. David's heart clenched with the fear that Ryan might never stir, that their shared dreams might evaporate like mist.

Beside him, David's parents shared knowing looks. They could see the profound love David held for Ryan—a love that had stood firm through trials and tribulations. It was a love they wholeheartedly endorsed, a love that had helped their son find his way back from the depths of despair.

David's father, a bastion of strength, fetched a chair from the corner and set it by Ryan's bedside. He offered it to David, who gratefully took a seat. His father's hand rested on his shoulder, an unspoken promise of steadfast support.

His Mum, her eyes glistening with tears, moved closer to David and enveloped him in a warm hug. "We're over the moon you've remembered, David. It's nothing short of a miracle."

David nodded, his voice a mere murmur. "I never want to forget again, Mum."

Together, they stood there, bound by love, hope, and the shared yearning for Ryan's recovery. Their silent understanding and unity filled the room.

Following their heartfelt embrace, David's parents decided to leave him alone with Ryan. They recognised his need for personal moments with the love of his life, a chance to convey his feelings and share the memories he'd regained.

As they headed toward the exit, David's father glanced back at his son, wearing a proud grin. "We'll be just outside if you need us, David. Take all the time you need."

David acknowledged their departure, his focus returning to Ryan. His parents exited quietly, leaving him in the serene confines of the recovery room.

David turned his attention back to Ryan, he leaned in, his words soft and heartfelt. "Ryan, it's all come flooding back—the love, the laughter, and even the pain. You've been my rock, my anchor, and the love of my life. Please, come back to me. I love you."

His words lingered in the room, steeped in profound emotion. David understood that the path ahead might be fraught with challenges, but he was prepared to face it head-on with unwavering love and resolve. Ryan was worth every battle, every tear, and every moment of uncertainty.

In the hushed serenity of the recovery room, David waited, his heart heavy with longing and hope.

As David settled in the waiting room, his hands were still trembling from the shock. The first thing on his mind was to notify his parents about what had happened. His fingers shook as he carefully retrieved Ryan's phone, which was still clutched in his unconscious lover's hand.

With urgency gnawing at him, David dialed his parents' number. His voice quivered as he spoke into the phone, "Mum? Dad? It's David. I need you to come to St. Thomas' Hospital right away. Ryan's been stabbed in the stomach. He's in surgery. Please, hurry."

Through the phone, his parents' concern was palpable. They assured David they were on their way and would reach the hospital as quickly as possible. David hung up and sat in the waiting room, his anxiety mounting with every passing second. The fear of losing Ryan was overwhelming.

Time seemed to stretch endlessly as David sat there, staring at the floor, lost in his thoughts. Suddenly, the entrance to the waiting area burst open. His parents rushed over, their eyes wide with concern and faces etched with worry. They didn't need words; their tight embrace conveyed their shared anguish. David clung to them, tears streaming down his face. He needed their support more than ever in this moment of crisis.

His Mum's voice was shaky as she asked, "What happened, David? Is Ryan going to be okay?"

David did his best to convey the situation, his voice trembling, "Ryan's in surgery right now. Elle got into our flat and started attacking me. Ryan got there in time and fought her, but she had a knife on her and stabbed Ryan. The EMTs got there quickly, but… it was bad."

His father's grip on his shoulder tightened, reinforcing their familial bond. "We're here for you, David. And for Ryan."

David nodded, appreciating his parents' unwavering support. He was grateful that they had arrived so promptly, just when he needed them the most. Together, they waited in the dimly lit waiting room, their collective worry creating an unspoken bond.

As minutes turned into hours, David couldn't help but reflect on the tumultuous journey that had brought him to this point. The memories he had recently recovered swirled in his mind, both painful and precious. The love he shared with Ryan had endured every trial and tribulation, and David clung to the hope that it would see them through once more.

Finally, a nurse emerged from the double doors that led to the surgical unit. David's heart leaped into his throat as he stood, his parents beside him, waiting anxiously for any news.

The nurse offered a compassionate smile as she approached. "You're here for Mr. Evans, correct?"

David nodded, his voice barely audible. "Yes, we're here for him."

The nurse proceeded to update them on Ryan's condition. "The surgery went as well as could be expected. The doctors were able to repair the damage and stop the bleeding. Mr. Evans is in the recovery room now, still unconscious. He's stable, but he'll need time to heal."

Relief washed over David, a weight lifting from his shoulders. He turned to his parents, tears of gratitude in his eyes. "He's going to be okay."

His Mum embraced him tightly, tears of relief mingling with his own. "Thank goodness."

The nurse continued to explain the situation. "You can see Mr. Ryan in a little while once he's settled in the recovery room. We'll keep monitoring him closely. He's a fighter, and we'll do everything we can to help him recover."

David thanked the nurse, overwhelmed by her kindness and professionalism. He knew that the battle wasn't over, but at least they had hope on their side.

As they waited for the moment when they could finally see Ryan, David realized that, despite the terrifying ordeal they had just experienced, his memories—both the pain and the joy—had brought him to a profound realization. His love for Ryan was unwavering and boundless, a force that could overcome even the darkest of trials.

The recovery room provided a moment of respite after the frantic events in the emergency surgery. Soft, gentle lighting bathed the room, and the steady, rhythmic beeping of medical gadgets added a touch of tranquility. David, flanked by his parents, couldn't help but feel a surge of relief and gratitude as they entered.

David made a beeline for Ryan's bedside, where his love lay in a deep slumber. Tubes and machines surrounded Ryan, a testament to the diligent care he was receiving. David took hold of Ryan's hand, feeling the reassuring warmth in his grasp. He leaned in closer, his voice filled with emotion. "Ryan, it's time to wake up. I've got my memory back, and I need you here with me."

Ryan remained serene and still, as if enjoying an afternoon nap. David's heart clenched with the fear that Ryan might never stir, that their shared dreams might evaporate like mist.

Beside him, David's parents shared knowing looks. They could see the profound love David held for Ryan—a love that had stood firm through trials and tribulations. It was a love they wholeheartedly endorsed, a love that had helped their son find his way back from the depths of despair.

David's father, a bastion of strength, fetched a chair from the corner and set it by Ryan's bedside. He offered it to David, who gratefully took a seat. His father's hand rested on his shoulder, an unspoken promise of steadfast support.

His Mum, her eyes glistening with tears, moved closer to David and enveloped him in a warm hug. "We're over the moon you've remembered, David. It's nothing short of a miracle."

David nodded, his voice a mere murmur. "I never want to forget again, Mum."

Together, they stood there, bound by love, hope, and the shared yearning for Ryan's recovery. Their silent understanding and unity filled the room.

Following their heartfelt embrace, David's parents decided to leave him alone with Ryan. They recognized his need for personal moments with the love of his life, a chance to convey his feelings and share the memories he'd regained.

As they headed toward the exit, David's father glanced back at his son, wearing a proud grin. "We'll be just outside if you need us, David. Take all the time you need."

David acknowledged their departure, his focus returning to Ryan. His parents exited quietly, leaving him in the serene confines of the recovery room.

David turned his attention back to Ryan, he leaned in, his words soft and heartfelt. "Ryan, it's all come flooding back—the love, the laughter, and even the pain. You've been my rock, my anchor, and the love of my life. Please, come back to me. I love you."

His words lingered in the room, steeped in profound emotion. David understood that the path ahead might be fraught with challenges, but he was prepared to face it head-on with unwavering love and resolve. Ryan was worth every battle, every tear, and every moment of uncertainty.

In the hushed serenity of the recovery room, David waited, his heart heavy with longing and hope.

31

Ryan

THE CONSTANT BEEPING got on Ryan's nerves at first. He couldn't figure out where he was or what was happening. His body felt all heavy and sluggish, like he was stuck in some slow-motion dream. But Ryan wasn't one to stay down for long.

With a determined effort, Ryan managed to open his eyes. The stark white hospital room came into focus, and he blinked a few times, trying to make sense of it all.

Then he saw it, or rather, him. David. His rock, sitting right by his side. Just knowing David was there made everything feel a bit less bewildering.

Ryan reached out, his hand trembling a bit, and ran his fingers through David's hair. It was a gentle touch, a silent way of saying, "I'm here."

David seemed lost in his own thoughts, not realizing Ryan was slowly waking up. But that touch, that connection, spoke volumes about their bond. It was like a lifeline, grounding them and reminding them of their deep love.

Ryan couldn't help but smile faintly as he met David's eyes. David sensed something was up, turned his attention to Ryan, and their eyes locked. In that moment, they didn't need words to understand each other. Their eyes said it all.

"I was so worried," David admitted, his voice thick with emotion. "I didn't know if I'd ever see you again."

Ryan's heart ached at the vulnerability in David's voice, and he gently shook his head, never breaking eye contact. "It would take more than a stab wound to keep me away from you," he whispered, his voice hoarse but full of determination.

David's eyes teared up with relief, and he admitted, "I love you so much," his voice shaking.

Ryan's smile grew warmer, and he reached out with his free hand to cup David's cheek, brushing away a tear that had slipped out. "I love you too, David," he said with tenderness. "More than words can say."

David moved closer, being careful of Ryan's condition. Their lips met in a soft, tender kiss—a kiss that spoke of longing, gratitude, and the deep love that had brought Ryan back to him.

As they pulled apart, their eyes stayed locked, and they continued to communicate without saying a word. It was a language of love, of hope, and of an unbreakable connection.

"I've got something to tell you," David whispered against Ryan's lips, his voice filled with hope and excitement.

Ryan's curiosity was piqued, and he couldn't help but feel a surge of happiness. He knew that whatever David had to share was significant—a testament to their enduring love.

"What is it?" Ryan asked, his voice barely more than a whisper as he held David's gaze.

David's eyes sparkled with newfound clarity, his expression radiating happiness. "I've got my memories back," he revealed, the words carrying a weight of joy that lifted his heart.

Tears of happiness welled up in Ryan's eyes, unshed but brimming with emotion. "David," he breathed, his voice choked with happiness.

He pulled David closer, enfolding him in a gentle embrace. "I'm so, so happy for you."

David returned the embrace, holding Ryan with a tenderness that spoke volumes. In that hospital room, they found solace and strength, knowing that their love could conquer even the darkest of times.

Their lips met once more, not in urgency, but in the sweet celebration of their love. It was a kiss filled with promises for the future, a future where they could build new memories together, free from the shadows of the past.

With each tender touch and whispered word, they reaffirmed the unbreakable bond that had brought them back to each other. In that hospital room, they found solace and strength, knowing that their love could conquer even the darkest of times.

Finally, their lips parted, but their gazes remained locked, communicating a depth of emotion that transcended mere words.

"I love you, David," Ryan confessed, his voice a soft, heartfelt declaration.

David's eyes shone with tears of happiness, and he leaned in to capture Ryan's lips in another sweet kiss before sleep took over him again.

Ryan's eyes fluttered open once more, pulled from the hazy embrace of slumber by voices in the room. The hospital room slowly came into focus as he blinked away sleep. There was a dull ache in his abdomen, but he was relieved to find himself awake and aware.

Turning his head slightly, Ryan saw that David and his parents were gathered around, deep in conversation with Detective Wayne. Wayne's presence in the room added a sense of seriousness, and Ryan's curiosity was piqued. What could they all be talking about?

Struggling to sit up, Ryan propped himself on the hospital bed, focusing on David, who noticed his awakening and made his way over. The worried lines on David's face softened when he saw Ryan was awake.

"Hey, you're awake," David said softly, relief and concern in his voice.

Ryan nodded, still feeling a bit groggy, but he had to know. "What's going on?"

David turned to Detective Wayne, who cleared his throat and stepped forward to address Ryan. "Mr. Evans, we have some major developments in your and David's case."

Ryan furrowed his brows, trying to piece together what he'd missed while he was out of it. He had no idea what had happened since his last moment of consciousness.

Detective Wayne explained, his tone serious but tinged with triumph. "We managed to catch Elle, the woman who attacked you. She's in custody now, facing attempted murder charges." He continued, revealing more of the twisted plot. "We also arrested her brother for his involvement in the hate crime against David."

Ryan was perplexed. "Her brother? But why?"

Detective Wayne's gaze was unwavering as he laid out the disturbing truth. "Elle ordered her brother to take David out of the picture. She pretended to be someone else, using text messages to manipulate the situation."

Ryan's mind was spinning as he absorbed the shocking revelation. Someone he'd once cared about, someone who had become a source of danger, had orchestrated this horrific act. It was hard to grasp the depths of Elle's malice.

Beside him, David looked equally stunned and troubled by the unfolding truth. Ryan reached out, taking David's hand, giving it a reassuring squeeze. They'd face this ordeal together, just like they always had.

David's parents, standing nearby, wore expressions of concern and disbelief. The room felt heavy with

the weight of the situation, but there was also a sense of relief that justice was finally being served.

Detective Wayne reassured them, "We have solid evidence against Elle, including her text messages and her brother's confession. They'll be held accountable for their actions."

As the Detective spoke, Ryan experienced a mix of emotions—relief that Elle had been caught, anger at her betrayal, and gratitude for the unwavering support of his loved ones. The ordeal was far from over, but at least they were one step closer to closure.

David leaned in, his voice soft but determined. "We'll get through this, Ryan, together."

Ryan met David's gaze, his heart swelling with love and gratitude. With David by his side, they could face whatever lay ahead.

In that hospital room, amidst the revelations and uncertainties, their bond remained unshakable. Together, they'd weather the storm and come out stronger, ready to embrace the future with hope and resilience.

32

Ryan

I T HAD BEEN A COUPLE OF DAYS since the hospital, and being back home was a welcome relief for Ryan. Each step he took through the front door was cautious and weary, a stark contrast to the confident strides he'd had before the terrifying incident.

David, his unwavering rock through it all, stood by the door with a reassuring smile, ready to catch Ryan if he stumbled. "Home sweet home," David said, his voice a comforting melody. He guided Ryan to the couch, a soft haven of comfort that seemed to beckon him.

Ryan, settling onto the couch with a sigh of relief, gave David a tired but appreciative grin. "I can't believe we made it through all that."

David chuckled softly, his eyes filled with a mixture of love and relief. "We're a team, Ryan. We can handle anything together."

Physical recovery was a daunting task, but David embraced it with determination. He helped Ryan with everything from changing bandages to making sure he took his medications on time. The physical pain was real, a constant reminder of the harrowing encounter, but their love and mutual support made it bearable.

"You're better at this than the nurses, you know." Ryan said.

David grinned, his touch gentle as he worked. "Well, I'm the best nurse in town, especially for you."

Ryan chuckled softly, his heart warmed by David's care. "I'm a lucky guy."

As they shared a tender moment, Tyson entered the room. He meowed inquisitively, as if asking what was going on.

David crouched down and scooped Tyson into his arms, hugging the little one close. "Meow," Tyson responded, his eyes seemingly filled with curiosity.

"Oh, Tyson," David said, his voice filled with genuine remorse. "I'm so sorry I forgot about you."

Ryan, who had been quietly observing their interaction, couldn't help but chuckle at the scene. "Don't worry, Tyson forgives you. After all, you're his favourite human."

David smiled, his heart lighter. "I promise I won't forget you again, buddy."

As they settled into a comfortable routine, their flat began to feel more like a sanctuary. The wounds, both physical and emotional, would take time to heal, but with each passing day, they drew strength from their love and the presence of their loyal furry friend.

Tyson, sensing their need for companionship and affection, curled up on the couch between them, purring contentedly. It was as if he knew that he played a crucial role in their healing process, offering comfort in his own unique way.

David leaned over and kissed Ryan on the forehead, his lips warm and tender. "We're going to get through this, Ryan. Together, no matter what."

Ryan met David's gaze, his eyes reflecting a profound trust and love. "I know we will, David. With you by my side, I can handle anything."

As the evening sun cast a warm glow over their living room, they found solace in the simple yet profound moments of togetherness. Their journey to recovery had only just begun, but they were ready to face it with courage, love, and the unwavering support of each other and their furry companion, Tyson.

Epilogue

THE SOFT MORNING SUNLIGHT STREAMED through the curtains, casting a warm, golden glow across the room. It had been a year since all the crazy stuff that had put David and Ryan's love to the test. David stood in front of the mirror, fixing his tie, and couldn't help but think about all the ups and downs they'd been through.

The trials for Elle and her brother had been a real emotional rollercoaster for David. Going to court felt like reliving his darkest moments. But with Ryan, family, and friends backing him up, they'd made it through. Elle and her brother had been given the punishment they deserved.

In the here and now, David took a deep breath, trying to calm his nerves. Today was his wedding day, something he'd only ever dreamed about. The thought of marrying Ryan filled him with joy and a pinch-me kind of feeling. He couldn't believe how far they'd come.

Just as David was about to head out to check on Ryan, his manager Nic walked in with a warm grin. Nic had been there for David through thick and thin, offering a friendly hand whenever needed.

"How you feeling, David?" Nic asked, looking concerned.

David let out a nervous chuckle, his tie still giving him trouble. "Nervous, Nic. Can't help it."

Nic chuckled back, his eyes filled with affection. "Totally natural, mate. It's a big day."

David nodded, checking himself out one last time in the mirror. He smiled at the guy staring back at him, knowing he was about to start a brand-new chapter with the guy he loved.

"And how's Ryan doing in the other room?" David asked, his curiosity getting the best of him.

Nic's grin got even wider when he talked about David's soon-to-be husband. "Ryan's a bit jittery too, but who can blame him? He's been pacing around like a caged tiger."

David chuckled, picturing Ryan in his mind. He'd always found Ryan's quirks endearing, a source of endless amusement and comfort.

"I'm so glad you're here, Nic," David said with sincerity, his voice laced with emotion. "You've been my rock through all of this."

Nic's gaze softened, and he put a hand on David's shoulder, reassuring him. "It's been a privilege, David. You're like a brother to me. Seeing you happy today makes it all worth it."

David's eyes glistened with gratitude as he gave Nic a warm hug. The support of friends had been a lifeline in his journey, and he was deeply touched by their presence on this special day.

As they parted, Nic had one last piece of advice. "Remember, today is about celebrating your love with Ryan. No matter what happens, cherish every moment."

David nodded, feeling a sense of calm wash over him. Nic's words hit home. Today was about their love, a celebration of everything they'd gone through and the bright future ahead.

With a final tie adjustment and a heartfelt grin, David was ready to leave the room and join Ryan. The nerves were still there, but they were overshadowed by a feeling of excitement and anticipation.

The moment had finally come, and David could feel his heart racing with a mix of excitement and nervousness. In the small, picturesque chapel, the soft strains of music filled the air, setting the perfect mood for their big day.

David's Dad, a rock in his life, stood proudly next to him. David couldn't have asked for a better person to give him away to the love of his life. His Mum, glowing with happiness, stood beside Ryan, someone she now saw as a son.

The chapel was packed with close friends and family, all here to witness the union of two deeply in love souls. White flowers adorned the pews, and candlelight added a warm, intimate feel to the place.

David's eyes scanned the room, and his breath caught when he spotted Ryan. His soon-to-be husband looked absolutely stunning in his white tuxedo, a picture of timeless elegance. A wave of emotions hit David as he took in the sight of Ryan patiently waiting at the altar.

Ryan met David's gaze, and they shared a smile that spoke of love so deep, words couldn't do it justice. David wanted to kiss Ryan right there, to show the world his love, but they both knew they had to wait for the right moment.

The minister, a kind soul who'd known David and Ryan for years, stepped up to start the ceremony. The room fell silent as he welcomed everyone and talked about the importance of the day.

"Ladies and gentlemen," the minister began, his voice soothing, "we're here today to celebrate the love between David and Ryan. A love that's faced trials and grown stronger with each day."

David's heart swelled as he listened to the minister. Their journey had been tough, but their love had always won, bringing them to this moment.

The minister went on, "Marriage is a sacred bond, a commitment to face life together. It's a promise of love, support, and never-ending dedication."

David's gaze stayed on Ryan's as he soaked in the minister's words. They'd faced hardships, but here they were, ready to make their vows before loved ones.

"David," the minister turned to him, "do you take Ryan as your husband, to cherish, love, and support, through thick and thin, for all your days?"

David's voice, filled with emotion, rang out clearly as he said, "I do." Ryan responded with a loving smile, tears of joy in his eyes.

Then it was Ryan's turn. "Ryan, do you take David as your husband, to cherish, love, and support, through thick and thin, for all your days?"

Ryan's voice, equally emotional, echoed through the chapel as he replied, "I do."

The minister, a comforting figure at this important moment, motioned for David and Ryan to step closer. His presence reassured them that this was a cherished moment, one they'd remember forever.

The moment was met with applause and heartfelt smiles from their loved ones, who'd shared in their journey and now celebrated their love. David felt a rush of happiness, knowing they were surrounded by people who'd been there through it all.

The minister continued with words of wisdom, reminding them of the commitment they were making. He talked about communication, patience, and unwavering support, and David and Ryan nodded, locked in a loving gaze.

Finally, the minister got to the part where they exchanged rings. David's hands trembled just a bit as he took Ryan's hand and slid the ring on his finger, a tangible symbol of their love and commitment. Ryan did the same, his voice steady as he made his vows.

With the rings exchanged, the minister declared them husbands and sealed the union with a heartfelt kiss. The chapel erupted in cheers and applause, celebrating the newlyweds with love and joy.

As David and Ryan walked down the aisle hand in hand, their smiles radiated pure happiness. They were starting a new journey together, filled with hope, love, and dreams yet to come true.

"I love you, David." Ryan said to him happily.

"I love you, too, Ryan. No matter what."

Afterword

Thank you for embarking on this journey through my debut novel. It's my sincerest hope that you've found enjoyment in the pages of "No Matter What." Your support means the world to me, and I'm immensely grateful for every moment you've spent with David and Ryan.

If you've found this story to be a captivating experience, I kindly invite you to share your thoughts through a review. Your feedback matters greatly and helps pave the way for future adventures.

Warmest regards,

Ken Sanchez

About the Author

Introducing Ken Sanchez, the visionary behind spellbinding M/M romance-fantasy worlds where love and magic entwine in a mesmerizing dance. With a heart devoted to the art of LGBTQ+ romance and an unbounded imagination, Ken is your guide to immersive realms he's painstakingly crafted. A dreamer who infuses passion into every stroke of his ink, he's conjured tales that not only enchant with fantasy but also stir the deepest emotions of love, taking readers on a spellbinding journey through his vivid narratives.

www.ingramcontent.com/pod-product-compliance
Lightning Source LLC
Chambersburg PA
CBHW012025110726

47995CB00005B/1129